Randolph Runner

Books by David Dvorkin

Fiction

The Arm and Flanagan

Budspy

Business Secrets from the Stars

The Cavaradossi Killings

Central Heat

The Children of Shiny Mountain

Children of the Undead

Damon the Caiman

Dawn Crescent (with Daniel Dvorkin)

Earthmen and Other Aliens

The Green God

Pit Planet

The Prisoner of the Blood series

       Insatiable

       Unquenchable

Randolph Runner

The Seekers

Slit

Star Trek novels

       The Trellisane Confrontation

       Time Trap

       The Captains' Honor (with Daniel Dvorkin)

Time and the Soldier

Time for Sherlock Holmes

Ursus

Nonfiction

At Home with Solar Energy

The Dead Hand of Mrs. Stifle

Dust Net

Once a Jew, Always a Jew?

Self-Publishing Tools, Tips, and Techniques

The Surprising Benefits of Being Unemployed

When We Landed on the Moon: A Memoir

Randolph Runner

David Dvorkin

Editing, print layout, e–book conversion,
and cover design by DLD Books
www.dldbooks.com
Editing and Self–Publishing Services

The mechanical man depicted on the cover was designed and built in the 19th century by Canadian inventor George Moore. You can read more about Moore and his invention here:

http://davidbuckley.net/DB/HistoryMakers/1893MooreSteamMan.htm

The public domain image is available on Wikimedia Commons.

ISBN: 978-1-7345636-5-8

One

On New Year's Eve 2037, the President of the United States, Donald II, smiled politely and raised his champagne glass to acknowledge the toast. In attendance were a few friends, a fair number of family members, and some government officials—toadies all, but what else could a man in his position and of his disposition expect?

The public celebration would be immense, but his wife had insisted on keeping the private one relatively small. It was, he thought, past time to replace her.

"Thank you all so much," he said, reading the scripted words hovering in the air in front of him. He read the lame joke that followed the introduction, smiling in response to the gales of forced laughter, thinking what fools they were, loving his power over them.

If only his father could see him now!

By which he meant his actual father, of course, and not the replacement—although at least he could have been sure of praise from the replacement.

It was Donald II's sixtieth birthday and the twelfth anniversary of his ascension to the presidency, and that power was limitless.

I'm the most powerful man in the world, he thought, the alpha dog of alpha dogs. I can do anything I want. I'll be president for life, and my son will be Donald III after me.

Next year, he would dump that oaf Wolfe and install young Donald as vice president. The kid was only 21, but the Constitution had ceased to be a problem years before.

Happily contemplating the future and the many years of fun, frolic, and big game slaughter ahead of him, Donald II brought his glass to his lips.

Before he could take a sip, he became aware of a disturbance at the entrance to the room. He set the glass down untasted and stared toward the doorway, frowning, disapproving.

There was a sound as if a clumsy waiter had dropped something heavy onto a wooden floor. There were many clumsy waiters in the place.

A dark red, circular spot appeared suddenly on Donald's forehead, just above the midway point between his eyebrows, and his head jerked backward as if in preparation for a sneeze. His body jerked again, twice, and then he leaned forward, all the way, until his face rested on the tablecloth beside the champagne glass.

The president fell, but the glass did not. Not a drop was spilled.

The audience watched with variously disturbed expressions, their own glasses still raised in the aftermath of the toast. They were waiting for the president to drink first. They kept waiting. But Donald II sprawled unmoving. A red stain appeared on the creamy white tablecloth under his head and spread inexorably in all directions.

The guests watched with no more motion than Donald now displayed and no more sound than he now made.

The silence was broken by the sound of a chair being pushed back. Vice President Hiram Wolfe, seated two places away to the president's left, separated from him by the stunned First Lady, rose to his feet.

He cleared his throat.

"Well," he said, "isn't this the doggondest thing? I guess I'm President of these United States now." He chuckled. "Sure as hell ain't president of any other United States."

He waited for laughter, but there wasn't any. The crowd was still stunned. Many still held their glasses up, although some had drained theirs already and were hoping for refills to sustain them. They were all making rapid calculations about the future.

"Now, some of you may be finding all of this a bit irregular," the newly minted President of these United States said. "I understand. I do. I understand that."

He looked over the heads of the crowd to the ballroom's exit. A tall, uniformed man stood there. His broad chest glittered with insignia of rank and other undeserved rewards given him by a foolish nation. This was General Henry Roberts McDowell Redgrave, dubbed by the media "Howlin' Hank," a nickname his adoring troops had quickly adopted but which he despised.

Redgrave nodded to Wolfe, indicating that everything was proceeding properly.

"Irregular," President Hiram I repeated. "But we'll all adjust to the new reality quickly. If you don't think you can, if you prefer not to be part of our new America, if you feel too much a part of the America of—" he gestured toward the cooling corpse

"—the old days, I won't hold it against you. You can simply leave right now and go back to your old lives."

There was hesitation and uncertainty in the room. Then a few people tentatively stood up. They looked around, gauging how many were with them. They looked questioningly at the head table.

"That's right," Wolfe said. "That's fine. Go right ahead. You're fine. Please exit through the main door, right behind you, where General Redgrave is standing."

Heads swiveled suddenly. There were startled looks as the crowd realized that the famous Howlin' Hank was there to support President Hiram. A few people who had stood now sat down again.

Wolfe chuckled.

Those who still stood, the remaining Donald II loyalists, headed for the exit, some looking worried, some frightened, some defiant.

Wolfe watched them, mentally ticking off names. The list was about what he had expected.

The now ex–First Lady was not among them. That surprised him. She was still sitting frozen in place.

Not bright enough to know what to do, Wolfe thought.

He looked her up and down thoughtfully. When Donald II had elevated her to First Lady, Hiram had been jealous. But quite a few years had passed since then, and Hiram decided that he could do better now.

"Ma'am," he said to her, "I think you should leave, too."

She turned her still pretty, stupid face to him. "Who? What?"

Wolfe gestured, and a young officer in dress uniform rose

from a chair farther down the table, helped the woman to her feet, and led her across the room to the exit.

General Redgrave had been standing in front of the door, waiting until everyone who wanted to leave was there. Once the former First Lady joined the crowd, he stood aside and let them push their way out. When all were gone, he pulled the door shut behind them and stood in front of it again, as though guarding the exit. He bent his head to one side, listening for something.

The remaining guests breathed a sigh of relief. But their breaths caught suddenly at a protracted rattle of gunfire from just beyond the door.

The sound ended. Redgrave nodded in satisfaction. So did Wolfe. The guests stared wide–eyed at the president and continued to hold their breaths.

"Now, then," the president said. "Let's begin our new era."

Later, after the body of Donald II had been removed and his blood wiped away, and the new president and his loyalists had left for the large public ceremony, which had been converted to a celebration of President Hiram's accession, Henry Redgrave finally left the scene of the coup.

He stood in the lobby just outside the ballroom. The bodies of the late president's supporters had been removed, although he knew that the city was by now filled with other dead people as the purge continued. He looked at the bullet holes in the walls and the blood and brains on the walls and floors and pondered the evanescence of life and similar edifying sentiments. Then he left the building.

Outside, there was still occasional gunfire in the distance. Now and then, a flash briefly lit up the twilight, followed a bit later by a heavy boom he could feel through his feet—a sign of some recalcitrant military unit being either brought to heel or eliminated. But the cleanup was already well underway. All had proceeded with great efficiency, a tribute to his meticulous planning.

Hiram Wolfe was a dolt, but he was a canny dolt, clever enough to understand that details should be entrusted to capable hands—in this case, those of General Henry Redgrave.

Clever enough, too, Redgrave mused, to outwit the dolt who had preceded him.

Redgrave felt the need to walk, to stretch his legs, breathe the humid night air, cleanse his palate, as it were, of the bloodshed. But it was miles to his house, and even if the distance had been shorter, it would have been inadvisable. The street in front of the restaurant appeared quiet and peaceful, but he knew that was due to the heavy presence of armed men controlled by him.

He gestured, and a convoy of vehicles appeared from around a corner and drove up to him. In the middle was a heavily armored sedan. Surrounding it were armored vehicles of various kinds. They bore powerful weapons and soldiers who carried stupendously homicidal guns and wore grim expressions. Other armed men walked beside the convoy.

They recognized him in the twilight. They nudged each other and pointed. He could tell from the movements of their mouths what they were saying. "Howlin' Hank! Look, it's Howlin' Hank!"

He waved and smiled while grinding his teeth.

An aide held the back door of the sedan open, and Redgrave climbed inside.

"Home!" he barked.

The convoy moved off slowly. The roadway trembled under its wheels. New potholes were added to the multitude already there.

Disgraceful, Redgrave thought. This city is the capital of an empire, in fact even if not in name. It should be a showplace, not a shabby embarrassment. Perhaps I can bully President Hiram into spending some money to fix the place up.

Not too much money, of course. The military budget must always take precedence.

The convoy drove through the mostly empty streets of Washington. The heavy vehicles rumbled past bodies sprawled on the sidewalks and over bodies sprawled in the street. The only live people the convoy encountered were Redgrave's own uniformed troops, personally loyal to him despite the oath to the Constitution they had all sworn when inducted, an oath that had been losing its power even before the coup of 2021. It had lost the rest of its power in the years since then.

Redgrave looked out the window at the armed figures growing indistinct in the dusk, and he nodded in approval. The chaos of the latest coup would settle down, and these streets would be safe again, but for now, a heavy hand was necessary to keep order. In addition to his own loyal troops, he saw occasional groups of heavily armed Hundred Star Flag paramilitary. One could never be sure about those fellows, but for now, he thought they were supportive of him, if not loyal in the way his troops were.

But eventually they'll have to be moved out, he thought. Can't have armed paras roaming the capital. Send them south. Get them started on their holy mission, their crusade. Maybe we'll get our hundred-star flag, or maybe the greasers will wipe them out. It's a win either way.

Home was blissfully quiet and empty. Only the staff awaited him, and they didn't really count.

Everything was clean, everything was orderly, a light supper awaited him, and his bottle of bourbon was ready.

Redgrave ate quickly and retired to a small sitting room with his second glass of bourbon to watch the evening news. He wanted to know if any self-styled journalists needed to be put down before they could make trouble.

He need not have feared.

He flipped randomly through the channels. Most of them showed movies or other forms of entertainment.

Mindless drivel, he thought scornfully. No one thinks deeply.

A few channels carried the giant presidential celebration, narrated breathlessly and adoringly. The object of affection had changed suddenly from Donald II to Hiram I, but the narration was the same as it would have been had there been no change. No one interrupted the evening's fare to announce the disruption at the top of the American government. No announcement was necessary. Only an utter fool could watch the celebration in Washington and not draw the obvious conclusion.

Perhaps a time-traveling visitor from the 20th century would have expressed surprise at how easily Americans had come to accept monarchy disguised as presidency and succession by assassination. Not Henry Redgrave. He knew his fellow citizens well. He knew they had always yearned for a king and were always quick to bow before authority figures and accept their proclamations, even while stoutly proclaiming their status as free men who bowed to no one. When Donald I had expressed last-minute hesitancy about his planned coup in 2021, it was Redgrave, then a young officer, who had assured him that the public would acquiesce quickly; he had been right.

It wasn't that Redgrave knew his fellow Americans through astute observation, for he was neither astute nor observant. Rather, he had absorbed wisdom about his native country by listening to the casual comments of Anton Moravec, a European military man with whom he had served years earlier, who was indeed an astute observer of America. There was much about Moravec that Redgrave resented, not least his recent remarkable ascent within the power structure of the new Europe. Nonetheless, Redgrave had acknowledged the value of the man's words and had absorbed them into his own worldview.

Still, Redgrave had left nothing to chance in the matter of the ending of the Trump dynasty that he had once helped establish. Knowing the enemy's weakness was one thing. Counting on it was another thing, and one foreign to Henry Redgrave. He had planned and prepared meticulously for the founding of the Wolfe dynasty. He had slept little for the last few days. He had monitored every detail of the plan.

And now, at last, he could relax.

He realized that he had finished his drink. Normally, he only allowed himself two, but tonight called for a small celebration in the form of a third glass.

Before he could call out, his butler was at his side with the bottle.

"Jesus, Randolph," the general said. "It's as if you read my mind."

The butler smiled ever so faintly. "No, sir. I lack that capability. However, I thought it likely that you had decided to indulge yourself in a third glass of bourbon."

"I think tonight calls for it. Don't you?"

"Oh, indeed, sir. This is a glorious night for America. It marks the beginning of our revitalization."

Redgrave welcomed the words, although the upper–class British accent in which they were spoken jarred with the sentiment the words expressed.

However, that was standard with the servants provided by Superior Domestics. Although they were an American company, they catered to an extremely wealthy clientele who had grown up watching British costume dramas on PBS and yearned for that gracious lifestyle, albeit with the comforts of modern life added. Oh, one could ask for a butler with an American accent, or even a Cockney one, but Redgrave suspected that no one ever did.

Certainly Bobby Bonaire hadn't. He had inherited Randolph and had been satisfied with him.

Thought of yourself as a true aristocrat, didn't you, Bobby? the general thought. Thought the money would last forever, no matter how you squandered it, didn't you? Your sister knew better. She got out when she could. And now I've got a whole houseful of SD servants that I could never have afforded if I'd had to pay full price, including this terribly British butler, while you...

What was Bobby doing now? the general wondered. Pouring his own drinks?

Redgrave raised his glass. "Rest in peace, Donald II," he murmured, "by the grace of God, President of the United States of America."

That wording was awkward. He had never liked it. Should he urge the new president to drop it and return to the older usage?

No, he thought, I need the churches for now, just as I need the oafish Hiram on the throne for now. Later, we'll see.

He swallowed a large mouthful of bourbon and water.

Too much water, he thought. As usual.

As if the butler had divined the general's discomfort over his accent, he said, "As an American born and bred, sir, I look forward to the reassertion of our hegemony and our swift expansion to a union of 100 states."

"Oh, yes. Of course."

The butler's presence suddenly made Redgrave uncomfortable. He set his half-full glass on the small table beside his chair and said, "That will be all."

The butler nodded and retreated, bourbon bottle on a silver tray perfectly balanced in his right hand.

Randolph had just reached the doorway when Redgrave fumbled for his glass and, made clumsy by lack of sleep, knocked it off the table.

The butler moved so fast that Redgrave saw not even a blur. He felt a strong wind. One instant, Randolph was at the door. The next, he was beside Redgrave, straightening slowly and carefully, holding the bourbon glass.

"Unspilled, sir."

The voice was as calm and even as ever, but Redgrave was sure he detected satisfaction in the butler's tone.

Randolph placed the glass back on the end table. "Will there be anything else, sir?"

"No more alcohol, that's for sure. But your speed, Randolph! How is it possible?"

"It's part of my design, sir. Buttling requires speed. Superior Domestics has no way of knowing the size of the house or the number of staff where their butlers will be working, so we are all equipped to cover a large amount of territory in the smallest possible amount of time. Whether I'm to be the only servant in a big house or supervising a very large staff in a very large house, I must be able to check everything and see everything and hear everything. My eyes and ears must be everywhere at the same time. Figuratively speaking, of course."

"I see."

"Moreover, sir, I am able to make the rounds of your, um, reasonably extensive grounds several times a night without that interfering with my duties inside the house."

"You do that? But my men patrol outside around the clock. They guard me very well."

"They do like to think so, sir, and it would be best to let them continue to think so. They're good boys."

"Well, yes," Redgrave said, feeling dizzy and thinking that he must have drunk more than he thought. "But do you really think you can guard this house more effectively than my men? They're superbly trained and armed. They operate as a team. They have equipment, communications—"

"And they get in each other's way."

Redgrave was both so surprised and interested that he didn't notice that his servant had interrupted him.

"They operate together, in unison, like a machine,"

Redgrave said.

"That may be the theory, General, but in practice, a real machine operating by itself does a far better job."

"Meaning you, specifically?"

"Yes, sir."

"But you aren't armed. You're just a—I mean, you were designed to be a servant."

The butler bent over slightly and lowered his voice, just as though he were a human confiding something to a fellow human.

"Superior Domestics doesn't like to advertise this, sir, but they are determined to protect their intellectual property. Competitors have attempted to kidnap SD servants in the past, presumably intending to reverse engineer their processors. I am equipped to make sure that no one can do that successfully."

He straightened up. "I'd just like to see them try, I would," he added, his accent slipping a couple of notches down the social ladder.

"I had no idea about any of that."

"You attention has been occupied with the much weightier affairs of state, sir."

"Yes. Indeed. Are all of you SD servants equipped that way?"

"Not yet, sir. I'm the first. In that regard, I suppose you could call me something of an experimental model. My charge is, of course, to buttle to perfection, but also to safeguard everyone in this household, whether human or domestic."

"Intriguing," the general muttered. "You have astonishing speed and great strength. Are you armed, in addition?"

"No, sir. I believe that there was some discussion at

Superior Domestics about that, but in the end it was decided to err on the side of caution and program me with all of the unarmed fighting skills known to man but not to build into me any kind of weaponry."

"I guess I understand their caution."

"But if I may say so, sir, I would very much like to have a powerful laser beam built into one of my fingers."

"Um," the general said.

"It would be so handy for quickly heating up water for tea or coffee or for boiling eggs."

"Yes," the general said. "I can see that."

The drowsiness that he had been experiencing a short while ago had fled. He was alert, thinking furiously, evolving new plans for the future. Happenstance had presented a solution to a problem that had bedeviled him for years.

Not happenstance, he corrected himself. Destiny!

"Do you think you could give me a demonstration of your defensive capabilities? Not now, of course. First thing in the morning, let's say."

"I should be delighted to, sir. Coffee at six a.m., as usual, General?"

"Yes."

Two

At about 6:10 the next morning, General Redgrave awoke to a gentle coughing. He opened his eyes to see his butler standing beside his bed, holding a steaming cup of coffee.

"I woke up at the first cough," the general muttered. "As always."

"Indeed, sir," Randolph said, not mentioning that he had been coughing at increasingly louder volumes since six o'clock before the sound finally penetrated the general's snores.

After a quick shower and a light breakfast, the general, properly uniformed, headed out into the cool morning with his butler in tow.

He had fallen asleep thinking, and he was thinking furiously now. He was afraid to hope, but the future seemed much brighter. At least potentially. It all depended on what happened next.

The grounds around the house were not extensive, certainly not as extensive as Redgrave thought appropriate for his status, but they would do for this morning's experiment. In particular, they were large enough to maintain secrecy. Redgrave wanted to keep all of this to himself for now.

He ordered his men to assemble on the far side of the house, out of his sight.

"Now, Randolph, let's see about this speedy running of yours."

Redgrave pointed at a large, very old oak tree about 100 feet away.

"I want you to run to that tree as fast as you can and bring back a leaf."

Randolph held out a leaf. "Here you are, General."

The wind had almost knocked Redgrave over. He had scarcely been aware of Randolph's movement, but apart from the wind, here was the leaf, and there were deep gouges in the lawn marking the robot butler's path.

The man rocked a bit, trying to catch his breath, while the robot looked on, concerned, not breathing at all.

"Was that unsatisfactory, sir? I can do it again."

"No, no. That's fine, Randolph. One test was enough. Now, then, I'd like you to show me what you would do if you discovered an invader on the grounds."

Randolph's face changed subtly. It was no longer mild and kindly. His eyes drilled into the general's. He stepped forward, hands reaching.

The general stepped back. "Not to me! Summon my men. They'll play the role of invaders."

Another powerful wind. Randolph had run off at full speed, leaving another trail of divots in the lawn.

The general looked at the grass sadly. He spent a lot of money on lawn care. This running butler business was creating unforeseen problems.

Randolph was back, trailing armed and uniformed men

behind him.

The men stopped a few feet away, looking bemused.

Randolph stepped up to the general and said in a low voice, "I assume I am to incapacitate but not kill them?"

"Of course! They're quite valuable. Do your best."

Redgrave raised his voice. "Men, when I give the word, I want all of you to attack Randolph—" he gestured at the butler "—and try to subdue him. Don't hold back. Hands, feet, teeth, guns, knives. It's your preference."

The soldiers looked at each other in amazement. Then they looked at the portly butler in his tuxedo, white vest, gleaming black shoes, and bow tie, looking at them beneficently. They laughed nervously and shifted about.

One of them dared to say, "But, sir—"

Redgrave silenced him with a glare. Redgrave's glares were famous and rightly feared.

"Now!" Redgrave barked. "Attack!"

They moved, but reluctantly.

One man threw a half–hearted punch at Randolph's head, but the butler's head was suddenly not there. He dodged the punch without apparent effort, scarcely seeming to move.

In return, Randolph punched the soldier in the solar plexus. His fist moved so fast that Redgrave couldn't see it, but he could see the soldier doubled up in pain on the ground, desperately trying to draw a breath.

Anger replaced reluctance in the man's comrades. They yelled and jumped on Randolph, punching, kicking, biting, stabbing. They would have been shooting, too, but they were afraid of hitting each other.

Randolph tried, but despite his best efforts, a few broken

bones were inevitable.

He stood for a moment in the middle of a pile of moaning, writhing men, carefully straightening his clothes. Then he stepped carefully over the fallen "invaders."

"With your permission, General, I will return to the house and fetch the medical personnel."

"Um, yes. Yes! Quickly!"

Again, the wind, and Randolph was gone. Again, the trail of divots in the lawn.

Damnation, the general thought. I wonder if different shoes would help.

The whimpering and crying were becoming annoying. Redgrave turned away and trudged toward the house himself. He was scheduled to meet with the president in the afternoon, and he needed to prepare. He also wanted to authorize the addition of a laser to one of Randolph's fingers as soon as possible.

Before he went to bed, Redgrave told Randolph that he would now be in charge of patrolling the grounds. Why waste money on the men he had been using? Clearly, Randolph, who didn't sleep and who had such murderous abilities, could handle both the inside and outside of the house.

"Thank you, General. I'm honored. This would make the finger laser even more useful. In case of armed intruders, I mean."

"Yes. Absolutely. I'll authorize it. Start tonight. I'm going to bed."

It was a quiet night. There were no intruders. Randolph spent the hours of darkness—as bright as daylight to him—strolling through the grounds and working on a project he had long had in mind.

Even while his senses were alert for intruders, Randolph wrote and stored in his capacious memory a manual of instruction for robot servants in a great house. What to title this manual? He considered *What Would Jeeves Do*, but then he realized that many might refer to the work by its initials, and that would lead to unfortunate confusion. He settled on *Randolph's Rules of Order*.

He envisioned the book as containing everything newly arrived SD servants, from the loftiest butler down to the lowliest scullery maid, would need to know. Every detail would be covered. It would describe precisely the place in which everything belonged, and it would give clear instructions for making sure that everything was in its place. If a robot can be said to experience pleasure, then writing this manual in his head was filling Randolph with delight. He felt that he was truly fulfilling his purpose.

At precisely 2 p.m. the next day, General Redgrave entered the Oval Office. He came to attention and rendered a snappy salute. "Mr. President!"

President Hiram Wolfe looked up from the computer screen in surprise. He had been playing a particularly devilish game of Solitaire and was just about to beat the machine. "What? What are you doing here? Is something wrong?"

"We had an appointment, sir. It's to discuss the selection of a vice president."

Redgrave glanced around. The room was empty except for the two of them.

He had expected a full raft of advisers. He had prepared himself for a contentious meeting in which he would represent the interests of the military branch of government, while the civilians would whine and complain and resist his choice for vice president—namely, himself. They would natter about the legally established order of presidential succession, and he would remind them that in accordance with Donald I's executive order of January 15, 2021, such laws were in effect only until discarded by executive decree.

He had hoped that some would continue to argue and that he would have to remind them of the recent fate of the supporters of Donald II. He had imagined their faces paling and their trembling voices trailing away into silence. He had relished the image.

He had expected the most serious opposition to come from the president himself, Hiram I, as he insisted on being called, who would be uneasy knowing that only the beating of his own heart would stand between the powerful general and the presidency.

Well, if there were no civilian advisers present, it would be a simpler matter: an argument between the general and the president, with no one else chiming in. Perhaps, Redgrave thought, it would be easier to convince Wolfe of his loyalty without those other voices adding confusion and distraction.

"Oh, that," Hiram said. "I was going to call you and tell you not to bother coming, but I forgot. I've already taken care of it. But since you're here, do you have any hints for playing Solitaire? This computer is a fiend."

"No, I'm sorry, sir. I don't. What do you mean, you've taken care of it?"

"My son. He's gonna be veep."

"You have a son?"

"Oh, yeah. That was a surprise to me, too. After the divorce, his mother changed her name and disappeared. Never heard from her again. I didn't even know she was pregnant."

"You were married?"

"Oh, yeah. When I was young and stupid. Kept it quiet because it would've played hell with my public image as a playboy and ladies' man. My voters always loved that."

Redgrave winced at the idea of this monstrous oaf as a ladies' man. What kind of ladies? the general wondered.

"Congratulations on having a son," Redgrave said. "I'm sure that must make you very happy. Oh, and I'm sure he's very happy to have such an important father, but—"

Hiram I laughed loudly, a booming sound that filled the Oval Office and grated on Redgrave's ears.

"Hell, the boy doesn't even know about me yet. The FBI only managed to track him down yesterday. I've had them working on it for a while, a few of them that I could trust. Kept it from Donald II. Who knows what he'd have done with that info, right? Kept it from you, too, didn't I?" He aimed his presidential glare at the general in a way that made his distrust of the military man crystal clear.

"You did a remarkable job of keeping it quiet, sir," the general said. "But you can't appoint your son vice president without the approval of both houses of Congress. Does the young man have any political connections?"

"Connections?" The booming laugh broke out again. "Hell, Redgrave, he manages a fast-food joint in Salina, Kansas. No, he doesn't have any connections, or experience, or background, or anything. That's just how I want it. I'm gonna mold my successor like clay."

He made vague motions in the air above the desk, presumably thinking that he was mimicking the actions of a sculptor molding clay.

"Screw Congress," he added. "You know they'll do whatever I tell them to. They even did that for Donald II, and he was a weak little turd."

"He was not a strong man," Redgrave agreed, buying time while he pondered the sudden change in the situation. This previously unknown son meant that he himself was now a step further from the presidency than he had thought.

"Mind you," Hiram said, "I did learn some things from working with Donald."

"Oh, yes? What sorts of things, Mr. President?"

"Oh, you know, stuff like watch your back, sleep with one eye open, keep your powder dry, put not your trust in princes."

"When will I get to meet the young man, sir?" Redgrave asked.

"Eventually," Wolfe said cagily. "He's not in Washington yet."

Mentally, Redgrave ran through the list of his contacts in the FBI and decided that none of them would be of use in this matter. "Good idea, sir. The enemy is everywhere."

"Oh, yeah. Don't you know it!"

"What about the current vice president, sir?"

"That jerk. He'll resign when I tell him to. He knows what'll happen otherwise. Are we done? I need to get back to Solitaire."

"As long as I'm here, sir, there is something else. As you know, the EU–China–Russia situation continues to be perilous."

"I had some kinda briefing about that this morning. They're fighting, right? I got that part."

Redgrave sighed mentally and wondered, as he had before, if he had made the right choice in suggesting a coup to the cabal behind Donald I in 2021.

It had seemed like a good idea at the time. The Democratic blue tidalwave election victory of November 2020—the bluenami, as the press had called it—had washed over the ticket from the top to the bottom, from the presidency and Congress to the office of dogcatcher in Podunk, Iowa. The Democrats were due to take over the country at every level in January, and the liberal wing was in full control of the Democratic Party. January would mark a sea change in American life.

Redgrave didn't really care about any of that. The Democrats could rebuild the social safety net using steel cables, and he wouldn't object. But he would object to any cuts to the military budget. That could not be allowed.

So when he, despite being still a fairly junior officer at that point, was asked by the cabal if there was any way to change the outcome of the election retroactively, Redgrave had come up with a way to do just that. The cabal had asked him to take care of it, and he had done so.

But as time passed, he had come to think that he had not acted wisely.

As Donald I's presidency became more monarchical and grandiose, Redgrave's influence diminished. Kingly displays increased. The military spending Redgrave had counted on went increasingly to parades and immense building projects designed to celebrate the glory of Donald I. Even though Donald I wasn't really Donald I, the cult of personality grew, encouraged by

Donald II, who planned to inherit the cult along with the office.

The orange blob's official death in 2025, while long overdue and not at all surprising, had not brought relief. His son and successor, Donald II, was an even greater dolt than his father. Redgrave had risen in rank and should have had even more influence, but he seemed in fact to have even less. The second Donald had brought in his own team of advisers, and Redgrave felt increasingly eclipsed.

He had counseled himself to play the long game. Events had seemed to prove him right.

Donald II had chosen an obscure congressman, Hiram Wolfe, as vice president. Donald III was only a teenager, and Donald II, in one of his rare departures from doltishness, had had the good sense not to appoint the kid as vice president. Wolfe would serve as a safe placeholder for a few years. Untrustworthy like all of his family, Donald II usually didn't trust others. He didn't trust Wolfe, but he didn't consider him dangerous, either.

Perhaps he would have been right if Redgrave hadn't ingratiated himself with Wolfe and planted dangerous ideas in his head. The result was the second coup, the one just completed.

Now all the Donalds were dead, Hiram Wolfe was president, and Redgrave was, or should have been, the power behind the throne. This previously unknown son of Wolfe's was a wrench in the works.

What do I know about this boy? Redgrave wondered. Nothing. Not even his name, except that it's not Wolfe. I know that he manages a fast-food restaurant in Salina, Kansas. Wolfe shouldn't have let that slip. I'll set my people on it. Meanwhile, to the business at hand.

"As you know, sir, the Euros and the Chinese are expanding into Russia, steadily eating away at its territory. So far, the Russians have hesitated to use their nukes, but at some point, desperation could set in, and they'll have no alternative. India is pretending to mediate, but I suspect that in reality they're just killing time, waiting to see who comes out on top."

"What do you think?"

"I think it's hard to say. Eventually, Russia will collapse, and then we'll probably see the China-India war we've all been afraid of. Maybe the Euros will try to pick up the pieces."

"Boom!" Hiram I said. "They'll all nuke each other. Radioactivity everywhere. Then *we* can pick up the pieces."

"They'll be too hot to hold. We're better off continuing to focus on the Americas."

Wolfe's own focus had drifted back to the computer screen.

"Sir!" Redgrave said. He was suddenly tempted to beat his commander-in-chief to death.

"Huh? Oh, yeah. Go on."

"Whoever wins over there, once they recover from the fighting and put everything back together, they'll have a huge advantage over us in terms of population and industrial base. Especially population. We need to control all of the Americas before that happens, but we don't have the manpower to do that."

"You've got that gang you use. Thousands of stars, or whatever."

"Hundred Star Flag. They're useful, but they're not worth much in the long run. No, we need an army of at least ten million real troops."

"Ten million!" Hiram I's attention was suddenly focused. "What the hell? We can't do that."

"We can, sir. I have a way to do it. It won't even cost much. You'll be commander–in–chief of the most powerful army in the world. That army will make you Emperor of the Americas."

Hiram gazed into space for a moment with a happy smile. "I like the sound of that. Do you think that would turn women on?"

"Women always like grand titles, sir."

"Okay. Write up what you need, and I'll sign it."

"Thank you, Mr. President."

Redgrave was opening the door to leave when Wolfe called him back.

"Oh, hey, I need you to do something for me. I want you to set up some kind of dinner party with those rich people you grew up with. You'll introduce my son, Eddie, to them. That's the first step. They'll talk him up, and then I'll announce him to the world. Tell me the date, and Eddie'll be there."

Redgrave swallowed his annoyance at being treated like a social director. At least now he knew the son's first name. His people might have enough to track the young man down.

"Certainly, Mr. President. And I'll have an Executive Order on your desk in a few hours, giving me the authority I need to create your new army."

"In a few hours, I'll be off duty. Drinking. Make it tomorrow."

"Yes, sir."

The president returned to his game of computer Solitaire, and Redgrave left.

Three

Eddie DeBeer loved his job. He loved the store he managed. He loved the people who worked for him. He loved his employer, Mama Johnson's Home Cooking, which owned a few thousand identical small fast-food restaurants across the country and which was in fact a very small ingredient in a giant, highly diversified, vile corporate stew, a fact that Eddie knew but wasn't bothered by. He loved his customers, even the ones who made his employees' lives hell and seemed to be trying to make Eddie's life hell as well, but unsuccessfully because Eddie loved them.

Eddie simply loved people.

It wasn't because he was a simpleton. Far from it. He was quite intelligent. His upbringing had been dreadful and would have done permanent damage to anyone else, but Eddie was quick to forgive and had a remarkable ability to look on the sunny side and pick himself up and dust himself off and move on with his life with a smile on his face. He was a sappy meme made flesh.

Understandably, a lot of people couldn't stand him. Eddie could tell. He responded by loving them, which usually made them utterly detest him.

So when two men in uniform entered his restaurant, he greeted them with a heartfelt smile and said warmly, "Two for lunch?"

Eddie was substituting for the hostess, who had phoned him that morning to tell him she was sick and would not be in. Eddie had seen through her immediately. It was clear to him that she just wanted a day off. He didn't care. He loved her, too. He had laughed and said, "Sure! Come back when you feel up to it."

His restaurant, inevitably, was deeply in the red and was about to be shut down by corporate headquarters, which was inhabited entirely by evil people who hated everyone, but Eddie didn't know that. He would have been hard put to change his management style even if he had.

"Are you Eddie DeBeer?" one of the men asked.

"That's me. Two for lunch?"

"Have you lived in Salina for as long as you can remember?" the other man asked.

"I have. Two for lunch?"

"Come with us."

"But, my restaurant—"

Before he could finish the sentence, the two men grabbed his arms and half carried him out of the restaurant and into a waiting car, which sped off immediately.

The fate of the restaurant is lost to history. Perhaps Eddie was replaced with someone more efficient and competent, which is to say much less full of love for all humanity, and it survived. Or perhaps Mama Johnson's Home Cooking shut it down and it was replaced by something even more synthetic.

Either way, its part in the life of Eddie DeBeer was complete, and it now fades from our story like the morning mist burned off by the rising sun, or perhaps some other similarly poetic and evocative image.

It was lunchtime and traffic was heavy, at least by Salina standards, but the other vehicles moved out of the way for the car Eddie was in, and it sped down the vacated lane at a speed considerably above the posted limit. Eddie glimpsed the faces of the passengers in the cars they passed. They looked surprised and annoyed as their cars obeyed a command the passengers had not given them.

Eddie asked all the questions one might expect: "Who are you? Where are you taking me? Why are you taking me? What's going on?" Occasionally he threw in, "I have to get back to work!"

The two men ignored him. He was in the back seat, with one uniformed man on either side of him. Both looked away from him and at the passing scenery.

They were now on I-135, headed south.

Eddie switched tactics. "Pretty, isn't it? I like it out here. How about you guys? How does it compare to where you're from?"

Silence.

"Is this going to be a long drive? Because I'll have to pee pretty soon."

No response.

"It's prettier if we turn east. Hillier, and more trees. It gets pretty flat if we keep going south. Right?"

One of the men snickered, briefly amused by Eddie's amateurish attempts at getting information out of them.

The other man said, "Enjoy the scenery while you can, sir. Relax. It will all be over in a few hours."

All be over? Eddie thought. While you can? Oh, God, what are they going to do to me?

He sat rigid, every muscle tense, while the car drove south to Wichita, then through Wichita, and then exited the freeway.

This is it! Eddie thought. They're taking me out into the boonies, and they're going to shoot me and bury me, and no one will ever know what happened to me!

Then it occurred to him to wonder why they would go to so much trouble. If they had wanted to kill him, why would they drive all this way before doing it? Anyway, why would anyone want to kill him?

Worst of all, whatever these men did or didn't do, there was no one who would wonder what had happened to him.

I've lived in Salina for as long as I can remember, he thought, filled with sadness, and no one there has ever cared one bit about me, except Mom, and she's dead.

He sat back in his seat, tears blurring his vision. The tears kept him from paying attention to where the car was going. Not that it would have made much difference, since he wasn't familiar with Wichita.

He was wrong about his mother. She, too, had never cared about him. She had fled to Salina, changed her name, and brought up her son, keeping him in complete ignorance of his father, merely because she despised her ex–husband. Her dying thought had not been to wonder how Eddie would manage without her but rather to gloat that she had won. Now that she was about to permanently vanish, the bastard would never be able to find his son. He'd probably never even know the boy existed. She wore a beatific smile as she stopped breathing.

Eddie, standing beside her bed, fighting back tears, said, "She's at peace. She's with the angels now."

The nurse looked up from the note she was writing and said, "Oh. Right."

Eddie came out of his mournful reverie as the car came to a stop in front of a barrier arm. They had stopped beside a guard shack.

All the car's windows rolled down simultaneously, and a uniformed guard looked into the car. One of the men beside Eddie held something up for the guard to see.

The guard straightened and saluted. He gestured to someone inside the shack. The barrier arm rose, the car windows rolled up again, and the car drove forward.

"Why haven't they automated this?" one of the uniformed men said to the other.

"I know," the other said. "Primitive boonies."

They had spoken to each other as though Eddie weren't present. Now they lapsed into silence again.

The car drove across what Eddie realized was an airfield. They passed aircraft of various kinds that Eddie couldn't identify. They all looked enormous to him. He wanted to get a better look, but he was afraid to lean forward. He wanted to ask questions, but he was afraid to do that, too.

Eventually, the car came to a stop next to a long, slender aircraft with stubby wings, parked in the blazing sun on a wide expanse of concrete. The aircraft had no markings. Its sides were smooth and gray, unbroken by windows.

The men climbed out and yanked Eddie with them. The car sped away.

The sun blazed down on them. Heat baked up from the concrete. The humidity was stifling.

Eddie looked around. "Where—?"

"Nowhere," one of the men said.

"Be quiet," the other one said.

"Sir," the first one added.

A door opened in the side of the aircraft and steps folded down, reaching the concrete.

"Climb," one man said.

"Sir," the other added.

"Right," the first man said. "Sir."

Eddie climbed the stairs and found himself in a small, windowless room containing a couch and two armchairs. It was cool and pleasant in the room. It wasn't pleasant for Eddie, who was terrified and really, really needed to pee.

One of the men pointed at the couch, and Eddie sat. The two men took the armchairs.

Eddie sensed motion. He thought they were moving forward, faster and faster, and then it felt like they were lifting into the air, angling steeply upwards.

"Back to civilization at last," one man said.

"Yeah," the other said.

They fell silent again. They stared into space.

Eddie looked around for something to read. There was nothing. He wondered how long the trip would last, whether he would be allowed to go to the toilet, if there was a toilet, where they were going, and most of all, why? That was the question he really wanted answered: Why? Also, why him? That was the other question he wanted answered. Also, what would happen to him? That was the question he wanted answered most of all.

There was probably no point in asking any of those questions.

He sighed, leaned back, closed his eyes, and tried to think calming, comforting, non–pee thoughts.

If they *are* going to kill me, Eddie thought, they're sure going to a lot of unnecessary trouble.

That was actually a comforting thought. He couldn't come up with any calming thoughts. Most of all, he couldn't stop thinking about peeing.

Four

Gunther Bonaire earned his money the hard, old-fashioned way: by scamming retirees out of their life savings. He was so successful at it that he retired early to live a life of nouveau riche gaudiness—modeled, to the extent a man with no inherent taste or sense of balance or proportion could do, upon the gracious lives of the restrained aristocracy depicted in British costume dramas, which he and his wife devoured on their local PBS station.

Gunther and a gang of other equally soulless and self-deceiving plutocrats bought up the tiny town of Hickdorp, Minnesota, where his ancestors had briefly lived, evicted the residents, leveled the town, and erected what they thought looked like a typical English village of long ago, but with modern plumbing, which they named Snootville.

The surrounding countryside was idyllic, with verdant hillsides, bosky dells, babbling brooks, and abundant animal life—although the animals, instead of admiring the lovely views, ate each other, as animals will.

Gunther and his evil fellows bought that surrounding countryside, scraped it, leveled it, sterilized it, and sold it to developers, who in turn landscaped it, built giant houses on it, and gave the area names like Misty Haven, Wildlife Meadows, Pristine Highlands, and so on. Soon the houses were filled with exceedingly rich families, and the huge attached garages were well-stocked with Chrysler Excessives, Lincoln Highbrows, and other such vehicles. Gunther and his pals and the developers made a killing.

Gunther had the sense to buy some of the lovely countryside and keep it unspoiled. He built a rather small house on the land. It was meant to be temporary. He was planning something much bigger and probably Georgian. Fate had other plans.

His son, Frederick, inherited Gunther's money and extreme Anglophilia but fortunately not his moral sense, or rather lack of moral sense.

After his father's early death, brought on by an excess of meaty dinners, rich desserts, and gin and tonic, Frederick moved to Silicon Valley and helped found a company called Superior Domestics, whose goal was to combine robotics and artificial intelligence in order to produce servants who would be like the fictional ones in those British costume dramas but notably superior to the human ones Frederick's father had repeatedly hired and fired while Frederick was growing up.

These robotic servants would be tireless, perfect, uncomplaining, extremely long lasting, and require little or no maintenance. They could also be switched off when not needed. The company's motto was, "All the gracious living of Upstairs with none of the unseemly drama of Downstairs."

The company's first models were a long way from the ideal Frederick and his colleagues had in mind. The computers inside their heads were very powerful, and SD's software developers were brilliant, but the robots' hardware was primitive and limited in comparison to the software. The servants SD produced could understand commands and respond appropriately, but through mouths that didn't move the way human mouths do. Their facial expressions were rudimentary and obviously not human. Their bodily movements were clumsy and graceless. They were enormously heavy; one would never invite them to sit down, and not just because servants shouldn't sit in the presence of their masters and mistresses. They had a distributed network of batteries throughout their bodies, but even so, they would run down after a few hours of sluggish activity and have to plug themselves into the nearest outlet for a few more hours to recharge. Their repertoire was limited; they could serve at meals, for instance, but so clumsily that it was safer to have real human servants perform those duties while the robots stood around looking impressive. In short, the early models, of which Randolph was the very first, were little more than extremely expensive decorations.

Still, they certainly were decorative, and they did make favorable impressions on potential customers. Sales were meager but just enough to keep the company going. In addition, the founders and owners of SD were sinking their own once impressive but steadily shrinking personal funds into the venture, shakily confident that they'd start making a reasonable profit before cash flow problems forced them to give up and shut the company down.

Ironically, increasingly, the company's real value lay in its brilliantly innovative artificial intelligence software and, later, its robotics hardware. They could have raised funds on those alone, but they didn't want to relinquish even a fraction of ownership in the company. They feared that if they let any of their intellectual property out the door, it would inevitably pass into the hands of competitors, and they would probably not become the super–mega–billionaires they hoped to be. They even hoped that they might become trillionaires.

Frederick was somewhat less optimistic than the others, perhaps because he wasn't part of the technical team and had little appreciation for what they had already accomplished. Moreover, his share in the company was much smaller than that of the others, and so he found it hard to anticipate stupendous wealth for himself.

The attempts to gain control of SD's valuable intellectual property increased steadily.

Numerous corporations, from very large to enormous, offered to buy SD for immense sums of money.

Government agencies asked, at first politely and then with increasing rudeness, to be allowed to use SD's technology.

Foreign governments tried to buy the technology and then tried to steal it. Indeed, the U.S. government and other corporations also tried to steal it. Just barely in time, SD upgraded its product with the deadly defense skills Randolph would later demonstrate to General Redgrave.

Intelligence agencies, both American and foreign, probed SD for a weak link. All of them quickly settled on Frederick. He was subjected to endless attempts at seduction by women of indescribable beauty and astonishing erotic power. It wore him down. More precisely, he was faithful to his wife, Marianne, and it was the constant fear that at some point he would snap and let himself be seduced that wore him down.

Forget trillionaire. Forget billionaire. He estimated that his share of the company was already worth a few million more than he had sunk into it, and he decided that was enough. He told his partners that he wanted to leave the company.

They agreed happily and bought him out for more than he thought his share was worth and far less than they thought it was worth or would eventually be. They threw in a dozen of SD's best products at no extra charge, including Randolph, on condition that they could visit his home at will to monitor their robots in action and to upgrade them as often as possible.

Out of Frederick's hearing, one of his cofounders said to another, "This could be risky. We've never tested an upgrade without people watching the robot's every move, and with all kinds of safeguards. Maybe there'll be a robot rebellion. Maybe they'll murder Fred and his family."

"All the more reason to do this testing far away from here."

"Oh. Good point."

Frederick took his donated servants and his few million dollars in profit and went home.

There was no robot rebellion.

The company continued to exist, improving its robots, selling small numbers of them, making pretty good money, but still worrying about cash flow.

Back home in Minnesota, Frederick told everyone he knew and every reporter he could find that he had been involved only on the financial side of the company and didn't know anything about its technology and now wasn't involved with SD at all.

He didn't stay in Minnesota for long. Now that he had money and time, he reasoned, why shouldn't he indulge his

Anglophilia?

Marianne didn't share Frederick's affection for all things English, despite her parents having emigrated from England to the U.S. before her birth, or perhaps because of that, so while he went off to tour the Mother Country (not actually mother to any of Frederick's ancestors, but he didn't care about that), she stayed behind in the rather small house Frederick had inherited, where at almost every turn she stumbled over a Superior Domestics butler or maid or footman or cook or whatnot propped against a wall and set to Sleep Mode. It freaked her out.

Meanwhile, Frederick explored the island of Britain from north to south and east to west. He loved everything he saw, and he swallowed every tale he was told.

In the north of England, he believed completely when an estate agent told him that the crumbling ruins he was gingerly stepping through—all that was left of an insignificant abbey destroyed in the time of Henry VIII—were the remains of Locksley Hall, where Robin of Locksley, later known as Robin Hood, had been born and reared.

"Are you kidding me?" Frederick said, gasping for breath in the cold, damp air, for he had inherited his father's tendency to portliness and poor cardiac health.

"Not at all, sir. And below us, although mostly filled with dirt now, are the dungeons in which the barons of Locksley imprisoned their enemies. It is said that the Sheriff of Nottingham once imprisoned Robin himself in these very dungeons, and he stayed there for many months, until he was freed by the great strength of his Merry Man Little John, who tore the chains from the stone walls and then broke the metal cuffs that were around Robin's wrists."

"Wow!"

"As it happens, sir, the Hall is on the market. The owners are in some financial distress and are hoping for a quick sale."

"Oh, my God! Do you think it would be possible to take it all apart and ship it back to America?"

"I'm sure that could be arranged. My brother owns a construction firm, and my cousin works in shipping. Shall I speak to them?"

"Of course! How wonderful!" Frederick cried, for he had inherited neither his father's business acumen nor his ability to judge character.

I've even got the land, he thought. Robin Hood would have loved it there. Dad's old house can become an outbuilding.

And so the ruins of the supposed Locksley Hall were carefully taken apart, all the pieces were labeled, and the whole was shipped to Minnesota, where the Hall was reassembled, with all the pieces that had been destroyed by weather and neglect replaced with modern substitutes. The result was a strange hodge–podge that would have bewildered the old monks even more than Henry VIII's abandonment of the one true church had done, but it matched Frederick's fantasies about medieval England.

The old stones felt at home in the humidity of their new home. The winters rattled them, but they kept their silence; they knew that overall they were better off. Also, they were stones.

As the new version of Locksley Hall grew in the exurban countryside, Marianne's waistline grew as well. It grew alarmingly. She was told she bore twins and that the birth would be a difficult one.

It was an awful one, a horrible one, an agony for the ages, a torture greater than anything anyone had ever suffered in medieval England. Or so she told people for years afterwards.

"But didn't they give you anesthesia?" people would ask her when she told the story of her agonizing birth experience, as she often did even without being asked, which didn't make her popular at parties.

"Yes, of course, but it didn't make any difference. It still hurt like hell!"

She often wondered why she had trouble keeping friends.

In the hospital, after she had finally, as she put it, expelled the two parasites, she told her husband, "You've got your heir and a spare. That's it."

"No more children?"

"No more sex."

Concerned, loving, he leaned over to give her a sweet kiss on her sweaty forehead.

"*Get away from me!*" she shrieked.

He did, quickly and—although he didn't yet know this—permanently.

He left her hospital room and wandered down the hallway to the viewing area, where new fathers could look through glass at their newborns.

Grace and Robert Bonaire lay side by side in a double-wide crib just on the other side of the glass.

Frederick gazed at them lovingly. They were perfect.

Grace was chubby and had slight fuzz on her head that a passing nurse told him would be flaming red in the very near future. She waved her little arms and legs and grinned happily— at him, Frederick was sure. Her brother was a bit longer and more slender, with darker features and black hair already showing on his scalp. He lay fairly still, staring somberly into space, contemplating the awful things life was planning for him.

A nurse came in and pressed a pad of some kind against the sole of Grace's foot. She repeated the process with Bobby. Both babies started crying and wriggling around vigorously.

Frederick couldn't hear anything through the glass, but he heard their cries of pain in his heart.

He banged on the glass.

The nurse looked at him, startled.

He shook his head and wagged his finger.

She squinted. She glared at him.

He dropped his hand to his side and stepped back, terrified.

Satisfied, the nurse returned to her work with the other babies.

Frederick wondered if the nurse would have responded to him subserviently if she had been a Superior Domestics robot. In time, he was sure, SD's product would replace nurses. He wasn't sure how he felt about such machines caring for his own precious babies.

Frederick loved his two kids unreservedly. He loved them more every day. To him, they were perfect little angels, except when they were being devilish, and then he loved them even more.

It delighted him to think that he would leave them his great estate, a place with room for both of them to settle down with their spouses and produce innumerable children of their own, creating a mighty clan of Bonaires, all of whom would revere him down the generations as the man who had given them Locksley Hall.

The original abbey had in truth had storage spaces beneath

it, but for wine and other consumables, not prisoners. The reincarnated building had extensive dungeons and secret corridors, where Grace and Bobby loved to play and terrify each other. The building was a magic place for them.

Frederick loved to tell his children stories about Robin Hood and Locksley Manor, some gleaned from reading, some invented by him on the spot. He considered the inventions to be harmless little fibs; if they instilled in his children a love for the family estate and an affection for England, then the fibs were justified.

Bobby and Grace swallowed it all until they were teenagers, at which time they would respond to their father's repeated stories by looking at each other and rolling their eyes. But despite their adolescent affectation of cynicism and their protestations to each other that they knew their father's stories were rubbish, the kids secretly believed almost every word of the beloved tales and continued to believe almost every word even after they had both grown to cynical adulthood and should have known better. Perhaps what they really loved was the special status the stories conferred on them.

Unlike Frederick, who could see no flaws in his children, Marianne could see little in them but flaws. She grew increasingly indifferent to him and to them. The Hall itself began to irk her more and more. Before long, she realized that she had married a fool, and one who, thanks to his obsession with the Hall, was no longer a wealthy fool.

Despite her increasing dislike for her two children, she felt a duty toward them. She would stay, for now. Perhaps when both children had left home, it would be time to make a final decision.

In the meantime, as the years passed, Superior Domestics technicians showed up frequently, unannounced, invited themselves into the Hall, and installed upgrades to the robot servants' software and hardware. The servants grew steadily more lifelike and competent. Randolph was in charge of the staff and ruled it with, literally, an iron hand—but, paradoxically, a hand that was also just, fair, and kind. One can't ascribe human feelings to them, despite their steadily improving AI brains, but in their own way, the robots did experience emotions of gratitude and even devotion in return.

The twins adored Randolph. As his software grew in power, he felt increasing affection for them. The kids often told each other that their parents were sad losers, and they were right. But if one ignored the parents, then Randolph, the staff, and the twins presented a picture of gracious, charming life that could have stepped out of one of the British costume dramas that had inspired SD in the first place.

That is, putting aside the clothing and the accents of the two human children. Randolph and the servants had the proper accents, and as time passed and their bodies became increasingly humanlike, they were supplied by SD with the proper clothing instead of merely having it painted on their bodies.

Aboveground, the rambling building had both space and need for Frederick's Superior Domestics servants. Marianne wasn't happy about the family's new home, but now that the servants spent their time ambling around the huge structure, waiting upon her every need and doing mysterious things in the darker recesses, she was reconciled to it. Her primary misgiving had been that the place would be impossible to keep clean, but the servants took care of that.

For the present, she focused her attention on inoculating her children against her husband's childish fantasies, with little success while they were children but with increasing effect, or so she thought, once both had survived puberty.

In reality, Bobby and Grace had learned to mislead both parents in order to maintain harmony at Locksley Hall.

During his teenage years, Bobby lost what little bit of boyish sparkle and sense of fun he had ever had. His shoulders drooped, figuratively and literally, under the weight of the Hall's financial problems. Inevitably, Frederick believed in primogeniture, and his will reflected that, so Bobby spent his time learning what he would have to do once he inherited sole responsibility for keeping Locksley going. His early assumption that he would live an easy life of leisure and luxury gave way to the knowledge that he would spend his days scrambling to pay the bills, and that he might even, just possibly, horror of horrors, unimaginable hell, have to get a job.

In the same way, Grace learned that her job would be to snag a wealthy husband.

As it happened, she had someone in mind, and not because of his moderately wealthy family, but because she genuinely liked him and thought that life with him would be exciting and fun. Alas, just like her brother, the young man grew more serious and somber with time. Grace had planned that she and her boyfriend, as she considered him, would go to college together, meaning that they would live together in a distant town far away from both families. Instead, her boyfriend sought and got an appointment to West Point.

High school graduation was the end of their relationship.

The conventional name of the graduation ceremony, commencement, was in itself painful to Grace. She didn't want the ceremony to end, for that would mark the termination of her hopes and dreams. For Henry, the ceremony seemed endless. He did see it as marking the commencement of his glorious future, and he couldn't wait for that future to begin.

Finally, the last event in the commencement ceremony was introduced. A member of the graduating class would read a poem she had written for the occasion.

She began:

> *Our dear, beloved Snootville High*
> *We leave you now with many a sigh.*
> *It hurts so much to say goodbye*
> *As we head off, our tears to dry.*

The poem had many, many more verses, but at that point, she broke down and, sobbing, fled from the stage.

Henry and most of his classmates took that as signaling the end. They tore off their robes, threw their mortarboards in the air, and ran from the hall into the sunlight and the future, whooping and hollering. A few stayed behind, sitting, wondering what came next. Among them was Grace, fighting to keep the tears in her eyes from spilling out.

Grace went off to college, anyway—a small state college, but even so, straining her father's financial resources almost to the breaking point—where she caught and released almost every boy fish in that little sea without finding one she liked half so much as the one who had swum away.

Bobby stayed at home and tried to teach himself accounting. He hated it. He cried himself to sleep every night, clutching a bottle of cheap booze. He was already sufficiently financially responsible not to buy the good stuff.

Stress and calories caught up with Frederick on the day Grace came home at the end of her freshman year. What would have been a subdued celebration was instead a subdued funeral.

"Mom," Grace asked Marianne, "what are we going to do now?"

The question surprised Marianne, who, although she had long looked forward to her husband's death, hadn't thought of it as requiring her to do anything.

"Just go on as before, I suppose," she said vaguely. "We have the Hall, and the servants, and... We'll keep doing whatever it is we were doing."

She turned away from her daughter and back to her email, which she had been checking when Grace asked her that question.

"Oh," she said, reading an email from a distant cousin she had long forgotten, expressing condolences and proffering an invitation. "I guess we're going to England."

"I can't go anywhere," Bobby said. "I have to stay here and—" he gestured around wildly "—try to take care of stuff."

"I meant your sister and me," Marianne said coldly.

Her son had started to resemble his father, physically and in other ways, and that made her regard him with growing dislike. Her daughter, on the other hand—pretty, bold, strong, athletic, courageous—was turning into a carbon copy of the girl Marianne deceived herself into thinking she had once been, and she almost loved Grace for it.

They left Bobby to his booze and bills and took flight to a

country Marianne was sure she could never love but which she was determined to at least like.

She didn't. She was the same dissatisfied whiner in England that she had been in America. She hated the weather, the crowding, the coffee, and the plumbing. She hated the cousin's house, which was small, ordinary, and lacking in servants human or robotic. She hated the cousin.

The cousin who, suddenly overcome with compassion for a newly minted widow, had invited her, quickly grew to despise Marianne and started hinting that the American relative should feel free to go back home at any time.

Grace was welcome to stay for as long as she wanted. Everyone in England loved Grace.

Marianne borrowed her cousin's car and went for a long drive in the countryside to think about things. She drove at high speed down the wrong side of the road and annihilated an oncoming family of three and herself.

Grace wept, genuinely and unreservedly. Her English relatives tried to comfort her. A visitor, a handsome young man who possessed a modest fortune, tried so hard that she fell in love with him and married him.

Suddenly, Grace realized that Bobby had no idea any of this had happened. She texted him, "I'm married! Also, Mother's dead."

"Okay," Bobby texted back. "'Grats."

In his defense, his troubles were still mounting, and he was particularly deep in a bottle of very cheap gin.

Grace's new husband was of a wandering disposition. Before long, thinking of faraway places and worn out by his energetic wife, he wandered away. His wanderings took him mountain climbing in the Himalayas, where he fell over a cliff and died—instantly, one hopes.

The grief Grace felt was again genuine, intense, and short-lived. It quickly gave way to anger at her late husband for having gone away at all and then for dying in such a stupid and preventable way. She resolved to choose more carefully the next time.

She didn't, though.

The fortune she now possessed seemed large to her. It would support her nicely if she avoided extravagance. She reverted to her maiden name and removed herself to the Continent, where she spent a year traveling around, gawking at ancient stones, trying to puzzle out plaques on monuments, having adventures that were occasionally mildly dangerous, bedding many men and a few women, breaking lots of hearts, and pondering the sorry state of the world.

In Eastern Europe, she fell in love with an ambitious military officer in the nascent EU army named Anton Moravec. Perhaps what she fell in love with was not Anton himself but rather his resemblance, in spirit more than body, to the young man she had loved in high school and had never forgotten.

Unfortunately, that similarity was deeper than she realized. Moravec's ambitions called to him even more strongly than did Grace's delightful body. In addition, another woman was involved. This angered Grace. She didn't believe in fidelity for herself, but she had always insisted on it on the part of her partners.

Like others before him, Moravec was swimming away from her. She wondered whether she would ever find a line and hook strong enough.

She almost threw in the towel, but then she decided she wasn't ready to give up on Moravec quite yet.

"What can I do to make you stay?" she asked him. "To make this permanent? To make you dump her and be entirely faithful to me?"

He became thoughtful. "Where do your loyalties lie?" he asked her. "With America or Europe?"

"Europe, of course," she said, although in truth, she had never considered the question before and wasn't quite sure what the truth was.

Moravec seemed skeptical.

"But most of all, with you," Grace added. If nothing else, she knew which of his buttons to push.

"Ah! Well, in that case, there *is* something you can do for me. It will resolve all of this and lead us both to a happy ending."

He told her what he wanted.

"Interesting," she said. "I bet I could do that. Redgrave. It shouldn't be too hard."

Moravec laughed. "Yes, Henry Redgrave. It might even give him a stroke."

"It's a deal."

Grace returned to America.

Where she discovered that in her absence, her brother had married and sired a daughter.

"Why didn't you tell me?" she asked in amazement.

"Oh, I don't know. Forgot, I guess. It's this place." He gestured around him, indicating the Hall and its grounds and the entire world, his gesture as wild and frantic as she remembered.

"It's driving me crazy."

"Sell it. It was a fun place to grow up in, but what's the point now? The suburbs are getting closer. The land alone must be worth a lot. I bet you could get a pretty good price for the place."

"The nearest suburbs are at least fifty miles away."

"Exurbs, then. Don't quibble. Do your wife and daughter a favor. Sell the place."

"It's the family estate! I won't dishonor our ancestors."

"Oh, Bobby! That's ridic—"

At that moment, her five-year-old niece, Tandy, black-haired like Bobby but in every other way just like Grace, rushed into the room, shrieking happily. She flung herself at her newly favorite aunt, and Grace forgot about her brother and the not-very-ancestral home.

Tandy's mother, Harriet, entered the room much more slowly and quietly than her daughter. She had met her sister-in-law for the first time just a few days before, and she was in awe of her—of her vigor, her vitality, the abruptness of her movements, her exuberance, the way she entered a room like an explosion of energy.

Tandy was already beginning to affect Harriet in the same way, and she could already foresee that by the time her daughter was a teenager, if not before, she herself would be relegated to the background, as though stored away in one of the Hall's many dark nooks and crannies. Only the robot servants would be aware of her presence, she thought. Or perhaps they, too, would ignore her.

"I meant to tell you," Bobby said, ignoring his wife's presence. "I sent out an email last night telling everyone that you're back."

"That's nice," Grace said, her attention focused on Tandy.

"One of the old gang replied that he has a favor to ask of you."

"Uh huh." Her giggling niece was of much greater interest.

"Henry Redgrave. Remember him?"

"Oh, God," Grace said.

Five

Henry Roberts McDowell Redgrave was born in 1990 into a long line of successful insurance salesmen. Some years before Henry's birth, his father had bought one of the few old remaining farmhouses near Snootville. The house was an echo of the Hickdorp that had been. It was cheap by Snootville standards. It was large, and his family was growing steadily. And, he hoped, the location would lead to his making valuable business contacts. He wanted to blend in by matching the automotive excesses of wealthy neighbors, but all he could afford was a Chevrolet Tryinghard. The car fooled no one, but it did provide reliable transportation.

The elder Redgrave believed that the secret to success was self-discipline, regularity, steadiness, and attention to detail. By his standards, he was fairly successful, so perhaps he was right.

Henry emitted his first cry—and one of the last, because he soon learned to keep his cries to himself—minutes after Grace Bonaire was expelled by her mother in the same hospital, Snootville General, and minutes before Bobby followed his sister, a coincidence of which all three infants were, of course, entirely unaware.

From the beginning, young Henry was a misfit in his family. Not because he liked to play with toy soldiers. That's common enough with young boys, although Henry started doing it before he could walk or talk. But it was unheard of in his family; no child in the Redgrave line had ever been known to show an interest in imaginary wars. Nor was it his physical precocity. It's true that he was physically advanced in a family marked by and proud of its physical ineptitude. However, his parents expressed the hope that he would grow out of it—rather, that he would grow into the clumsiness and lumbering awkwardness common to Redgrave men. What really set him apart was his singular lack of the one attribute that all male Redgraves had shared for as long as anyone could remember: He cared not one whit about insurance, and when his father tried to initiate him into the sacred mysteries by reading to ten-year-old Henry the first few paragraphs of a whole-life policy, the boy threw up and ran away.

The father snarled to the mother, "That boy will come to no good!"

Perhaps events proved him right. Perhaps they proved him wrong. It's a matter of opinion.

In any case, from that point on, his father acted as though Henry didn't exist, concentrating his energies instead on Henry's numerous older brothers, who would sit cross-legged on the floor in front of his chair in rapt attention as he regaled them with stories of the clients he had reeled in and the occasional really big ones that got away.

Taking their cue from their father, the older boys also ignored Henry. When they did deign to notice him, it was to slap him, punch him, bite him, or kick him.

Henry absorbed this brotherly affection silently. He understood that this sort of attention was to be expected when one was part of a brutality of brothers. He waited.

Meanwhile, he grew in height, in breadth of shoulder, in depth of chest, and in circumference of arm. While his brothers pored over insurance policies and textbooks and basked in their parents' love, Henry lifted weights, ate as much beef as he could stuff into himself, and played violent games with like–minded friends.

Came the day when one of the brothers hit Henry and, at long last, Henry hit back. It only took one punch. The older brother, eighteen at the time, ran away screaming and crying like an eight–year–old.

It was morning, it was the first day of a new school term, and Henry had been about to leave for school. He thought about pursuing the other boy and finishing the job, but then he decided to indulge in the pleasure of anticipation. He would complete the destruction of his brother's face after school.

He hefted onto his back his backpack, weighted with overpriced schoolbooks, and headed out for Snootville High at a dead run. He was sixteen and had a driver's license, but he had no car, and he preferred to run everywhere because it increased his fitness level. He wanted to always be ready, physically and mentally, to fight. One never knew when the beloved homeland might be invaded by Russians, or Chinese, or Cubans, or older brothers.

He ran happily, easily, breathing regularly, a broad smile on his face. He reached school fifteen minutes early and fell in love.

Actually, he fell in love fifteen minutes later.

The quarter hour after he arrived and before the bell rang he filled with the usual foolish, testosterone–filled banter with his equally tall, equally muscular, equally violent friends. Then he noticed the time, cut the banter short, and headed into the building and to his first class.

It was American History, a subject he loved, especially the parts about war, and he had been looking forward to it eagerly during the recent break.

He chose a desk at random—he was one of those boys whose choice in desks teachers tend not to question—sat down, put his textbook on the desktop, opened it to the first page of Chapter One, and looked around with a smile.

That's when he fell in love.

Or what passes for love in teenage boys. You might call it lovelust. Whatever you want to call it, it was the first time it had hit him, and it hit him hard.

He stared at the girl in the desk immediately to his right, and he kept staring.

At the front of the room, the teacher began talking. Henry ignored him and kept staring.

At first, the girl responded to Henry's attention with a brief smile of her own, but she quickly grew annoyed and uncomfortable as he continued to stare.

Henry was aware of her response, but he couldn't help himself. He kept staring.

She was short and compact, with flaming red hair and a bright, alert face. Energy seemed to radiate from her. Everyone in Henry's family, and especially the women, was turned inward, carefully shut within an impenetrable shell. This girl aimed outward, and Henry was shot through.

He came to his senses enough to tear his eyes from her and aim them forward, but he was still watching her, or trying to, with his peripheral vision. The teacher was impressed with the boy's apparent fierce attention to his lecture and decided immediately that this fine young man would be one of his top students. It was the first of many undeserved positive marks Henry would receive throughout his academic and military careers.

After class and for the next few schooldays, trying to impress the girl, Henry engaged in foolish hijinks more suited to a boy two or three years younger. Given that his social development in relation to the opposite sex was at least that far behind that of other boys, this wasn't surprising.

She laughed, but eventually Henry realized that she was laughing at him in a derisory manner, not an admiring one. He switched immediately to a grave demeanor, copied from his parents. It was unnatural for him, but he was good at assuming a manner appropriate to the occasion and designed to impress others—a talent that would stand him in good stead in the future.

To this, Grace (because of course the girl was Grace Bonaire) responded. She wasn't quite sure why herself. She thought she preferred adventurous, exciting boys, but in reality her inner self sought stability and strength—in short, a man the very opposite of her father and brother, both of whom she loved dearly but could not respect.

With time, Henry's fascination with Grace became adoration, and Grace's moderate liking for Henry became... Well, let's call it love. Certainly it was a fairly powerful version of what passes for love in teenage girls. We can't call it lovelust;

perhaps breathlesstingly will do.

Grace started making plans for post–high school life.

She and Henry would go to some state university, where they would live together and eventually get married. Or possibly they'd get married right after they graduated from Snootville High. She hadn't made up her mind on that point. The only thing that was clear was that she would make that decision. Her parents would not be consulted, and neither would Henry. The two of them would major in dull, stable subjects and would lead dull, stable lives for many decades until they died, preferably at the same moment.

Perfect, she thought.

But Henry, despite his adoration for Grace, was falling in love with another powerful, dominant force: the United States Army.

It wasn't that he was intrigued by the possibility of being allowed to kill great numbers of people in foreign countries with impunity, although that idea did have much appeal. To his own surprise, however, his family's genes had started to assert themselves. Increasingly, what attracted him about the Army was its aura of stability, predictability, and certainty. Those were precisely what Grace wanted in her life, but the dull future she envisioned repelled him. The Army, he thought, would give him all that, plus excitement.

Simply joining up wasn't good enough for him. He didn't want to start at the bottom, at the first rung of the lowest ladder. He wanted to go to West Point and start at the bottom rung of the higher ladder.

Henry hadn't yet learned to keep absolutely everything to himself. He had become accustomed to sharing his hopes and dreams with Grace, but he knew he couldn't share this one with her. Instead, he confided in another boy—not really a friend, for he had none of those, but one of his fellow participants in mayhem and violence.

"West Point?" the other boy said. "You?" He burst out laughing. "With your grades, and your record, and the way you act? Never gonna happen." He laughed and laughed and laughed.

Henry knocked the boy down, removing two of his front teeth in the process.

Nonetheless, the incident made him thoughtful. The other boy had had a point, even though the kid would never be able to enunciate it clearly again. Henry's grades were deplorable, his behavior reprehensible, and his record abominable.

But I'm still a freshman, Henry thought. Maybe I can change things in time.

He was far from stupid. What he lacked was self–discipline. He had controlled himself when he wanted to impress Grace, and he was sure he could do so again. He was determined that, no matter how he felt inside, he could behave in a way that would impress his teachers, and he could raise his grades so that he became the top of his class. As for his record, well, he couldn't change the past. He would just have to hope that those in authority would so admire him for changing himself that they would forgive his past.

On the bright side, none of this would require that he purge himself of rage toward the world and contempt for those with power over him. Indeed, he could nurture his rage and contempt. He just had to keep both well hidden.

He read as much as he could about the service academies and was struck by the importance they placed on football. His first reaction was fury that they would squander taxpayer money on such nonsense. He wasn't a taxpayer yet, but he would be. He already felt that it was his money they were squandering.

It was an opening for him, though.

The football coach at Snootville H. S., noticing Henry's size and violent tendencies, had tried to recruit him to play for the school. Henry had dismissed him with a sneer—a sneer behind which lurked such violent rage that the coach had taken a step backward, while at the same time wanting the boy on his team all the more.

The idea of playing football did have some appeal for Henry because it seemed to him to be an approved, entirely permissible way to hurt other boys. However, he knew that it required showing up for practice and following orders, both of which he despised. But the Army would require the same of him, he reasoned, so wouldn't it be a good idea to start getting used to it now? More important, if he were to excel at the game at the high school level, it might outweigh some of the failings in his academic record in the eyes of the U.S. Military Academy at West Point.

And so one day after school, Henry showed up for football practice, making glad the heart of Coach Buddy Barron, whom the boys on his team called Beery Barron, but only behind his back. Buddy had been a minor star on the football team in his small high school and then had played mostly the bench position on the team at his state university. After being told to go away when he tried out for a professional team, he had ended up as a losing high school coach, bouncing from job to job, drinking too much, and constantly fearing that the current losing season would be the end of his tenure at his current school. But looking at Henry Redgrave, looking up at him, calculating the width of his shoulders, evaluating the murder in his eyes, Buddy began to feel just a little bit of optimism.

Buddy skipped the tryout and assigned Henry to the most violent, hard–hitting position in football, middlethudpucker, relegating the surly, stupid boy who had been playing that position to the bench. The boy looked at Henry and stifled the objection he had been about to voice. The bench suddenly looked appealing.

The only advice Buddy gave Henry before he played his first game was, "It's fine to injure players on the other team. It's actually a good thing. But do it so that the ref doesn't see. You see, son, that's how it is in life. Break all the rules and legs you need to or want to, but just make sure no one knows you're the one doing it."

Buddy's gamble paid off.

Thanks to Henry Redgrave, the team's fortune turned around. Leaving a trail of broken limbs behind him, Henry led his high school team to the state championship game. They would have won the game and the championship if the opposing team hadn't had two players as psychotic and murderous as Henry. They avoided Henry during the game, and he avoided them, but they injured his teammates so grievously that soon he was the only player left standing on his side. Of course he couldn't win the game by himself, but his photo and descriptions of his on–field exploits were front–page news all the way to West Point, New York.

Much the same thing happened in Henry's junior and senior years, except that both of those times, his team won the state championship.

Buddy's gamble had paid off, and so had Henry's.

The member of the House of Representatives for Henry's district was a graduate of Snootville High. The man had wept with joy when his beloved Snootville reached the state championships and then with bitter grief when the team lost the championship game. But as for Henry Redgrave, "What a man!" the congressman kept saying, shaking his head in awe. "I mean, boy."

When his office received a request from Henry for a nomination to West Point, the congressman wept for joy all over again and nominated Henry immediately.

The officials at West Point, thinking about future Army–Navy games, dashed a very few manly tears of joy from their own eyes when Henry's application was received. It was all smooth sailing from there.

After Henry graduated from high school, his erstwhile football team lost every game. Buddy Barron was fired, took even more heavily to drink, and died soon after of liver failure.

Thus it happened that, years before he met him, Henry was already following Anton Moravec's advice. "Clever leaders," Moravec would later tell him, "know the value of using sports to make their subjects think they're just like them. You must learn to do that, Henry. Americans love sports as much as Europeans do. The only difference is that your sports are even stupider than ours, but that's of no matter. The stupidity of the masses is the same. And don't worry about the bones and lives you break along the way. That's just part of the game."

When it came, the inevitable day was deeply painful for Grace but little more than a bother for Henry. He told her he would be going to West Point, not to the state university with her.

She wept and pleaded. He grew increasingly annoyed. The lovelust that had struck him at first sight of her faded almost entirely in minutes.

Adaptability was one of his strongest characteristics, and an important one for a man on his chosen career path. Her pain would last for quite a while. His would soon be a memory, an occasional moment of wondering if he had made the right choice, but nothing more than that.

At West Point, it was understood that Redgrave would try out for the football team. He did so and was quickly added to the roster, once again playing the position of middlethudpucker.

Redgrave played well but in a restrained manner throughout the season. He was saving his best for the crucial Army–Navy contest. There he would be his true self. That way, he reasoned, he would make the most powerful impression possible on the school's staff.

The game between the two service academies began, watched by thousands of people in the stadium and many more on television.

This was Redgrave's moment. He set out to maim his opponents and break as many of their bones as possible. He racked up a bunch of ribs, an arm, and a leg, the last two belonging to the same Navy player.

But the college game was different from the high school one. According to the rulebook, which the game officials quoted angrily to the Army coach, "A middlethudpucker may not break more than two minor bones per game, and then only in the second half and when his team is at least ten points behind."

Henry was benched. His team was severely penalized and lost the game.

Henry jumped up and down on the sidelines, howling in rage. His teammates, who had first resented him and now despised him, dubbed him Howlin' Hank. The nickname was not meant as a compliment. Henry knew that and raged internally whenever he heard it.

He left the football team soon after that first game and concentrated ferociously on academics. He did sufficiently well that he was able to stay at the academy for the whole four years.

Henry graduated from West Point and was commissioned a 2nd lieutenant, as was normal. He was assigned to mind–numbing desk duties in Washington and quickly began to think he had made a mistake. He would give the government the required five years of service and then get out of the Army.

The months and then years ground by. From time to time, he wondered what Grace was doing. Something much more interesting, he was sure.

He made 1st lieutenant when he was 25 and captain two years later. He was assured that this was perfectly normal; he was right on schedule.

That was the problem. He wanted to be gloriously ahead of schedule. He wanted to rocket to the top. He wanted to be a general. He wanted to be Chairman of the Joint Chiefs of Staff. Hell, he wanted to be president.

Itching for something more interesting than his current assignment, Redgrave was able to get himself attached to a United Nations peacekeeping mission in the Central African

Republic.

At last, people were shooting at him! Unfortunately, he wasn't allowed to shoot back. His role was limited to training other people to shoot at people. He was more frustrated than ever.

He was one of the very few Americans on the mission. There was also a small sprinkling of Europeans. Most of the troops were from African and Asian countries. Henry had absorbed a deep racial prejudice from his parents. He had also absorbed from them a deep distrust of Europeans, but he was desperate for companionship and began to spend much time with Anton Moravec, a Czech officer of his own age who was, infuriatingly, already a major.

Moravec was also erudite, charming, and multilingual. His English was perfect. So was his French, which many of the locals could speak. But that wasn't good enough for Moravec, who quickly mastered the local African language and was soon conversing happily in it with the people of the area. They were always happy to see him, chatting rapidly with him and plying him with food and drink. The children crowded around him, laughing at his jokes, looking at him adoringly.

Redgrave, meanwhile, was invisible to them. Even the few who spoke some English seemed uninterested in speaking it with him.

What was the man's secret? What was the source of his power over others? Redgrave had no idea, but he yearned to have it himself.

Moravec was also an amoral cynic with ambitions as great as Henry's own. "You say you want to be president," he said to Henry. "I have the same goal."

"President of the Czech Republic?" Henry sneered. "You have more power here and now."

Moravec shook his head. "President of the European Union. No, make that President of Europe."

"There isn't such a thing," Henry said. "You have a president of this and a president of that. They're all just competing with each other, and they're all weaker than the leaders of the big countries in the EU. There is no President of Europe."

"There will be."

"Even if there is, you're just a glorified trading association." Henry sneered again.

Moravec smiled. "That's true now. France was weak and at war with itself before Napoleon took over. Or Germany before Hitler, Italy before Mussolini, Spain before Franco."

"So you're going to be Napoleon with a swastika?"

Moravec shrugged. "Power first, ideology later. Perhaps some day we'll have a summit meeting, you and I. The President of the United States and the President of Europe. Two immensely powerful men deciding the fate of the world."

"Damn," Redgrave muttered, his imagination fired.

Moravec laughed.

Redgrave hated that laugh, and yet he admired it, too. In that short, simple sound, Moravec was able to express confidence, strength, and command. In secret, Redgrave would spend quite a bit of time trying to imitate it, but he never succeeded.

Six

Henry Redgrave resented Barack Obama for his brilliance, his blackness, and his erudition, and so in 2016 he voted for Donald Trump as representing the complete opposite. Redgrave was also voting against Hillary Clinton, who made him very uncomfortable. Perversely, he quickly came to despise Trump for his stupidity and ignorance and to think that he probably should have swallowed his distaste and voted for Clinton.

Sometimes he wondered how Trump could possibly have been elected. How could 60 million of his fellow Americans have voted for the fellow? Redgrave knew what had motivated him to vote for Trump, but what had motivated the others?

Perhaps he had forgotten a conversation with Moravec. Perhaps one would better call it a lecture by Moravec, for Moravec did tend to lecture Redgrave, who, despite their being the same age, had far less understanding of the world and always seemed to be in the position of the junior.

"You must understand, Henry, that somewhere around a quarter to a half of the population of every country are monsters. Inside, they boil constantly with anger, bitterness, resentment, envy, and simple, irrational hatred. They may direct it at Jews, blacks, foreigners, Roma, rich people, the homeless, and so on and so forth. The choice of target varies and never makes any sense. All that matters to them is that they have a target. A wise leader must always be aware of this."

"So that he can calm those feelings and keep the peace, you mean."

"Oh, no! So that he can determine which buttons to push and which targets to present to the violent masses. His goal is not to calm the feelings but to tap into them, to encourage them, to use the animal fury of the mob to sweep him into power and keep him there."

"Don't you believe in anything, Anton?"

"Certainly. I believe in Anton Moravec."

On the bright side, Redgrave was pleased that the risk of a major war increased significantly during Trump's first term. Wars represent opportunity for junior officers. Perhaps, Henry thought, he would get a chance to shine after all.

He did get that chance, but not in the way he expected.

After Africa, Redgrave found himself back in Washington, back behind a desk, and back to going crazy with boredom.

He volunteered for duty in the White House Military Office as a Social Aide, thinking he would make valuable contacts during his occasional evenings at the White House. He was accepted, at least in part because he looked good in his dress uniform. He liked the glamor of those evenings and the sense that he was at the center of power, but he soon realized that he was nothing but a glorified gofer.

One evening, while grumpily fetching coffee and late-night snacks from the kitchen for a visiting foreign dignitary, he passed two presidential aides in whispered conversation. He slowed down and perked up his ears, thanking the gods for his extraordinary hearing.

"She won't stay here," one whispered. "New York only, she says."

"What about Dee Eye?" the other whispered.

"He's no help. He's scared of her."

"We've got to have her here. Really bad optics if we can't roll her out for a big event now and then."

"I wish we *could* just roll her out, like a machine."

"And switch her off the rest of the time."

"Dee Eye would probably like that, too."

Redgrave had no idea what they were talking about, but instinct told him it was important.

"Gentlemen," he said, "perhaps I can help. It's what I'm here for."

They spared him a glance of contemptuous dismissal, but then they looked again. Redgrave was tall, handsome, and imposing in his uniform, but it was more than that. He had always had the good fortune to appear honest, honorable, and highly intelligent. He was not the first two, but history is made by what appears to be true and not by what is, as Moravec might well have said. On second glance, they decided to trust him.

"It's the First Lady," one explained. "She hates Washington and the White House. She's determined to stay in New York. We could keep her out of sight there, but we really need her here."

"Now and then," the other one said. "For public occasions from time to time."

"And maybe a brief speech or two," the first one added.

"Roll her out like a machine," Redgrave said, "and switch

her off the rest of the time. That's what you were saying."

"You heard that?"

"I hear everything."

Now they saw what they had missed before: Redgrave was intimidating, frightening, and dangerous. In this, they judged correctly.

"Have you heard of a company called Superior Domestics?" Redgrave asked.

Both men shook their heads.

"They're out in Silicon Valley. They make robot servants for the very rich."

"Robot servants? How come we've never heard of them?"

"You're not rich enough."

"But the president—"

"Isn't rich enough, either. Only real billionaires know about them."

A bigger reason they hadn't heard about the robot servants was that the robots weren't very good yet, as Redgrave knew perfectly well. There was no reason to mention that.

"I have a personal connection to the founders," Redgrave said.

Also untrue, or at least stretching the truth, and also irrelevant.

"For a price," he continued, "I'm sure they'll provide you with a robot that would satisfy your needs. Let's call her MM, for Mechanical Melania. Which reminds me, who's Dee Eye?"

"Oh, um, it's our pet name for the president. Letter D, Letter I. It stands for Donald the First. Roman numeral, you know."

Actually, it stood for Donald the Incompetent, Donald the Insufferable, and many other variations, but they weren't willing to share that with Redgrave yet.

One of the men asked, "What's in it for you?"

"Promotion," Redgrave said promptly.

The man shook his head. "We don't have that kind of pull. That's up to the Defense Department. Sorry. You'll have to stay a...whatever you are."

"Captain. Okay, then, how about making me a military aide to the president?"

The man shook his head again. "You need a higher rank than you have."

"Among other things," the other man said.

Redgrave was looking a lot less intimidating.

"Well, fuck, man, anything other than this crap." Redgrave held out the coffee cup to illustrate the crap. "Something important."

"You help us pull this off, and we'll see what we can do."

While Redgrave had no connection to the founders of Superior Domestics, he had once had a connection with Grace Bonaire, but we have seen how that ended badly. Her father, who was after all one of SD's founders, had seemed fond of Redgrave, but Frederick was dead.

What was he to do?

He continued with his food–and–beverage–delivery mission, mulling over the situation. His instincts still told him that this was a golden opportunity, but he couldn't see a way to capitalize on it.

He thought up and dismissed a variety of impractical plans. In the end, he was left with Bobby.

The way Redgrave remembered it, Grace's brother had

always been friendly and had seemed to like the possibility of Redgrave becoming his brother–in–law. Bobby was weak and useless and had no connection to SD other than being the son of one of its founders, but he was all Redgrave had, and Redgrave was desperate to capitalize on his new opportunity.

He dug up the number and made the telephone call.

A smooth, pleasing male voice answered in a British accent. "Lockwood Hall. Randolph speaking. How may I help you?"

Randolph? Who was Randolph? Then Redgrave remembered the mechanical man with a tuxedo painted on his body that he had encountered at the Bonaire home. How could he have forgotten the thing's clumsiness? If that was SD's best, then his big idea for advancing his career was worthless.

In the old days, Randolph's voice had been entirely mechanical, quite inhuman. This must be a human replacement. Not that this human servant spoke with much feeling, either.

"I'd like to speak to Bobby, please," Redgrave said. "This is Henry Redgrave, an old friend."

"Of course, sir. I remember you quite well."

"You remem—? Wait, you're not the same robot Randolph who was there years ago, are you?"

"I am indeed, sir."

"But you sound so—"

"So much more human. Yes, sir. I've had quite a few upgrades since those days."

Redgrave's spirits soared. "Excellent! Is Bobby available, Randolph?"

"I shall fetch the master for you, sir. One moment, please."

The master, Redgrave thought. He chuckled.

"'Lo?" It was Bobby's voice, as funereal and filled with

hopelessness as Redgrave remembered.

"Bobby! How wonderful to talk to you again. Henry Redgrave. You remember me, right? I was engaged to your sister."

"You used to hit me."

"No, I didn't."

"On the arm. Every time."

"I—"

"It still hurts."

"Really? Still?" Redgrave felt a rush of pride but tried to keep it out of his voice. A wave of pleasant boyhood memories swept over him. Now, in the maturity of full manhood, he knew of so many more arms that needed punching. He suppressed such thoughts and said, "Well, I'm very sorry, Bobby. I was just a mean kid, I guess. Some kids are like that, I'm afraid."

"You weren't a kid. You were a young man."

Jesus Christ! Redgrave thought. Will you stop being such a wimp? No wonder I used to punch you in the arm. You're lucky you're not within punching distance right now.

"Gosh, Bobby, what can I say? I've changed a lot since then."

"You dumped Grace. You broke her heart."

Redgrave winced. "We can't change the past, I'm afraid," he said, speaking from his own heart for a change.

"What do you want?"

"Mainly to see how you're doing. For old times' sake. I often think about you and wonder how you're getting along."

"Really? I'm surprised. Well, for your information, I'm not getting along very well."

There followed a long recitation of Bobby's financial

problems, his worries about the repairs Locksley Hall needed and that he couldn't afford, and the noisiness of the servants.

"They clank," Bobby said. "In the middle of the night. Harriet hates it. Just like my mother used to."

Who's Harriet? Redgrave wondered. That wimp has a girlfriend? A wife? Good God.

"Yes, I remember that about your mother," Redgrave lied. "Randolph answered the phone. I didn't hear any clanking."

"They experiment with Randolph. They keep coming by and upgrading his hardware and software. He's part of their R&D. Their other models aren't as good."

"By 'they' you mean SD?"

"Superior Domestics. Yeah."

"So you're still in touch with them."

"Sort of. It was part of the deal my father made with them when he retired, I guess."

"Are they going to upgrade their other models to match Randolph?" Redgrave asked.

"They would if they could, but they don't have the funds. They're self-funding, so they can't move ahead as quickly as they'd like. They're afraid that some giant company with lots of resources will leapfrog them any day now and put them out of business. It's a shame, too. They're light years ahead of anyone else."

"Hmm," Redgrave said. "They need money, and so do you. And your wife doesn't like the robots. I think I can help you both."

Redgrave made a quick trip to Minnesota to visit boyhood scenes, wax nostalgic, ponder the path not taken, wallow in old sorrows and pains, and all the other things we do to torture ourselves with the past. Then he shook himself out of that mood, something he had always been very good at, and talked Bobby into signing over to him ownership of all of his SD robots in return for a sum that was absurdly small but that Bobby foolishly thought was very big and would eliminate his money worries forever. Redgrave didn't possess that kind of money, but he was sure he'd be able to pay Bobby eventually. If not, well, too bad for Bobby.

Then—and this was the real point of the trip—Redgrave had Bobby introduce him by telephone to the SD principals, who listened to his proposal with a skepticism that changed rapidly to enthusiasm. They invited him out to their plant.

He was in Silicon Valley early the next morning. He met with the men who owned SD, professed himself astonished by their company's prowess in AI and robotics (he really was, despite himself), promised them funding he had no authority to promise, and obtained their promise to provide the special-purpose robot he needed in under a month. He was a good enough judge of men to feel quite sure that they would keep their promise and to feel equally sure that they were not very good judges of men.

He usually avoided praising others, except when he was trying to flatter them. However, he was so struck by the ability of SD's robots to read and listen in multiple languages that he spoke his mind. "You have a lot of powerful software crammed into those heads."

"It's even better than you think," one of the men said proudly. "We've distributed a lot of the processing power. All of their visual abilities are actually taken care of right in their eyes.

Same thing for interpreting what they hear. It all happens in the ear."

"Interesting," Redgrave said. "Those could be whole separate product lines—ears and eyes for people with hearing and vision problems. Even normal people. I'd like to be able to read a foreign language or hear it and understand without having to learn it."

The men looked at each other wide-eyed. Then they managed to hide their sudden excitement until Redgrave had left.

He wasn't paying attention to them, anyway. His thoughts were centered on his own bright future.

After that, tired but still driven, Redgrave flew back to Washington, where he used his old combination of synthetic charm, bluff manly heartiness, bullying intimidation, and knowing just which buttons to push to secure the funding he had promised SD.

And then finally he went home, to find that Bobby's domestic robots had already been delivered, and that Randolph, who was now much more human than the mechanical man he remembered from years ago, could easily be taught to prepare Redgrave's favorite drink, bourbon and water—although the robot insisted on putting in more water and less bourbon than Redgrave wanted.

Mechanical Melania was delivered one day before the date SD had agreed to. She was not entirely convincing, in Redgrave's view. She was just a little bit too robotic. But she sufficed, smiling stiffly and delivering vapid remarks in a halting manner that one aide told Henry made her seem more human than the original. Indeed, the aide said, Dee Eye actually preferred her, especially at night.

Whatever her shortcomings, MM earned Henry enough points to keep him in the White House, although he was still a mere captain and still essentially a gofer.

To make matters worse, no longer a gofer for visiting world leaders, he now fetched and carried for the two aides whose overheard whispered conversation had set him on his new path. They were both named John and might have been twins. They were certainly indistinguishable to Henry, who addressed them both as John, eschewing the surnames he had quickly forgotten, assuming that the appropriate John would respond.

Time crawled by. Henry made every effort he could to be noticed by Trump, who seemed to have a particular liking for manly men. Henry couldn't be sure if Trump remembered him from one encounter to the next, though. The president was such an indefinite, vague creature. He was generally human in form but ill–defined, more an orange blur of seething rage and resentment than a man.

MM had seemed to be a career breakthrough for Henry, but nothing significant had followed. His frustration was increasing. His rage was almost equal to the rage of Trump himself.

When DI was impeached in early 2020, Henry hovered as near to the fuzzy orange center of power as he could, but he was not called upon. He remained a captain and a gofer.

Of course the Senate made quick work of the impeachment

process with a meaningless trial, returning the expected acquittal. Nonetheless, Trump shrieked angrily that his stooges should have managed to avoid a trial completely.

The shriek stopped suddenly. One of the Johns rushed from the Oval Office, looking around wildly. He caught sight of Henry Redgrave and beckoned frantically to him.

Redgrave entered the Oval Office. This was his first time inside the famous room, the office he yearned to someday occupy as president.

He stopped in his tracks and looked around, awed despite himself. What drew his eye most compellingly was a floor-to-ceiling statue of Trump, posed heroically in a toga and with a laurel wreath on its head. The jaw jutted out, the eyes gazed piercingly into the distance, and the arms rippled with muscles. Redgrave's awe disappeared, and he stifled a laugh.

His examination of the place was cut short by the sight of an orange blob sprawled on the presidential seal in front of the HMS Resolute desk.

"Something happened to the president," one of the Johns said. "I think he's had a stroke."

"I think he's dead," the other John said.

"Get a doctor," Redgrave said.

"Can't," the first John said. "No one can know he's had a stroke."

"Or that he's dead," John Two said.

"Christ," Redgrave said, "you're all worthless."

Dead men had never bothered Redgrave. Even the first dead man he had seen, in Africa, hadn't bothered him, and he had seen many since then. He checked for a pulse.

"Yep," he said. "Dead. Fetch the vice president and... Who

swears him in?"

"Don't look at me," John One said.

The other John shook his head.

A man with an unfortunate beard stepped out from behind the statue and moved away from its shadow.

"Dee Two!" one of the Johns gasped. "We didn't notice you."

"No one ever does," the First Son, for it was indeed he, said bitterly. "But never mind that. Let's hold off a bit on swearing in the veep."

"You have something in mind?" Redgrave asked.

"We're the only ones who know Dad's dead. If he's not president, the rest of us are zeroes."

Henry stifled his first response. "Do you know about MM?"

"That's exactly what I was thinking," the First Son said. "You're the guy who suggested that, aren't you?"

"I am."

"Could we pull it off?"

"Superior Domestics keeps improving their technology. Besides, Mechanical Donald should be even simpler than Mechanical Melania. It would only have to keep repeating a few phrases, like, 'Many people say.'"

"And 'beautiful,'" John the First said.

"And 'no collusion,'" John the Second said.

"You catch on quickly," Redgrave said. "The secret couldn't be allowed to go much beyond the four of us. Oh, and of course the First Daughter, the Second Son, and the First Son-in-Law."

"Fuck them," Dee Two said.

Redgrave was beginning to warm to the man. He liked his devious way of thinking. Moreover, he saw an opportunity for himself. "I'll handle it all, sir. Of course, I'll want a promotion, and I want to be your personal aide."

"Done."

Dee Two glanced at the two Johns, who looked confused, and then back at Redgrave. The glance said clearly, "What about them?"

Redgrave smiled and nodded. Without speaking, he was saying, "Leave *that* to me, too."

Dee Two grunted. That meant, "It's a deal. I'm in your debt."

You mean you're in my grip, Redgrave thought.

Dee Two pointed at the body. "What about that?"

"There's a huge freezer in the basement, sir," John One said. He seemed more agitated than the situation warranted. Perhaps he was aware of his mortal danger and was trying to prove his usefulness. "The cooking staff store food in it."

"Interesting," Redgrave said, eyeing both men.

"It's really old," John Two said, talking nervously. "They used to use ice to keep it cold in the old days. It's full of lots of old stuff that no one even knows is there."

"In the back, he means," John One said. "The front part is full of frozen French fries."

"Perfect," Redgrave said. "Wrap the dead president in a carpet and take him away."

"Us?"

"Who better? *Now!*"

Redgrave might be a desk jockey, but he had a parade-ground voice when he needed it, and it did the trick.

The two Johns hurriedly wrapped the dead man in a presidential-seal carpet. One of them left the room and returned with a luggage cart. Sweating, gasping, moaning, grunting, and whining, the Johns heaved the 500-pound weight onto the cart and wheeled it away.

Soon the corpse of the never-really-elected 45th president of the United States was nestling comfortably at the rear of an immense walk-in freezer, next to the icebound rear leg of an elephant rumored to date from the time of Teddy Roosevelt.

Seven

Redgrave, now a major and Donald II's right–hand man, was remarkably busy. He was increasingly worried about the upcoming election and spent much more time than he liked in strategy meetings. During what time he could spare, he tried to lay the groundwork for his own future.

For a while, he had been adding newly minted young officers to his staff. In this, he was heeding advice given him years earlier by Anton Moravec, who had told Redgrave to surround himself with followers who revered him and would die for him if necessary. Much as Redgrave hated the man, he had never dismissed his political abilities. Moravec could have written a book of political advice to rival Machiavelli's.

Unfortunately, so far, Redgrave's new subordinates seemed to see their jobs as mere stepping stones and not as destinations. They didn't revere Redgrave. He wasn't even sure they liked him. He wanted to inspire devotion in them, but he had no idea how to do that. There were days when he fantasized about shooting the lot of them and replacing them with a new batch.

He tried not to think about the young fools and to turn his

attention to the outside world. He must start emerging from the shadow of the Trumps and make the name Henry Redgrave well known in its own right.

To that end, he contacted anyone he thought could help him get his name before the public. His effort was hampered by the dislike he had created in so many people, rising to disgust in many and blazing hatred in a few. He was surprised by how few people wanted to do him a favor. He had thought that everyone admired him as much as he did.

Still, there were a couple of people who hadn't yet seen through him, who took the pretense of bluff, hearty, manly determination at face value. One of them called someone he knew, who called someone he knew, who called someone else, and so on. The result was a request that he visit the studios of a local television station for an interview.

"To be shown during the evening news?" Redgrave asked, managing not to let his voice reveal his excitement.

"No, probably in the morning on a weekday," the voice on the phone said.

It was a start. He looked forward to the day when he would be able to order the execution of everyone who had treated him with insufficient respect.

"You must be prepared to bide your time," Moravec had told him. Redgrave was prepared to, at least somewhat.

"But you must also be prepared to strike while the iron is hot," Moravec had said. "To see an opportunity and seize it."

There were times when the man's remembered advice seemed more trite than brilliant.

I'll make my own opportunity and seize it, Redgrave thought. I'll make the iron hot and strike it. I'll impress them so much in this interview that they'll fall in love with me.

That wasn't quite what happened.

At the station, in a small, cramped, cold little room, he was interviewed by the station's rising star, Ariadne Felicity, the beauty of the newsroom. She was the opposite of Grace Bonaire in just about every way: black–haired, dusky, slender, intense, sharp, closed off, mysterious.

The lovelust she inspired in him was just as intense and instantaneous as that inspired in him by Grace in high school, long ago. It was something Henry Redgrave hadn't felt since those days. Because of his intense career focus, it was something he hadn't even thought about since splitting from Grace. Now, suddenly, he could think of nothing else.

His lovelust made him lose his ability to think clearly and speak coherently. He stammered and mumbled his way through a disastrous interview. He was aware of Ariadne's growing contempt. Her questions became ever more sarcastic. His answers became ever more incoherent.

At last, he was released. He stumbled into the parking lot, his uniform soaked with sweat, his cheeks aflame with humiliation, his penis thoroughly engorged.

Moravec had said, "A wise general knows how to turn defeat into—"

Anton, Redgrave thought, shut *up*!

He was drowning in depression. He was convinced that he had blown his one chance at greatness.

As it happened, he was wrong, for Ariadne, misunderstanding her audience, overplayed her hand. She saw the interview as an opportunity for her to rise above local television news and become a nationally known journalist. To hell with all those fan letters from locals. They often arrived damp, anyway—soaked with saliva and possibly semen, she suspected.

Rather than air the interview, she set about writing a probing profile of Henry Redgrave, one which would thoroughly expose the incompetence of the White House staff, and which she would try to get published in *The Washington Post*.

She dug into Redgrave's background. She uncovered his high school relationship with Grace Bonaire, a name she had heard from friends in Europe. She looked at photographs of Grace, sneered, and threw them aside. Then she investigated Redgrave's career at West Point. His grades there were better than she had expected, so that avenue seemed closed. Apparently, he wasn't incompetent.

Fortune struck, or so she thought, when she turned to Redgrave's athletic record. She dug up online messages about his violence on the gridiron. She fixed on the story about his breaking bones in the Army–Navy game, his being thrown out of the game, his howling from the sidelines, and the resulting Howlin' Hank nickname.

She tracked down one of his victims from that game, the owner of the arm and leg Henry had broken. She found a broken man, terrified of the name Redgrave even now, a man who had dropped out of the Naval Academy after that game and, after regaining the use of his two limbs, had begun a lifetime career as a stock boy.

This was gold!

"The Violent White House! How the questionable promotion of bloodthirsty junior officers has made the seat of government a hotbed of violence and incompetence and endangered our national security. Take Henry Roberts McDowell Redgrave, for example."

Something like that. She'd probably eliminate the exclamation mark in the title. That would be more suited to a less sober publication than *The Washington Post*.

The whole thing, as she wrote it, was unsuited to the sober *Post*, but the editors liked the substance of her story. It was rewritten, toned down, published under her byline, and took the world by storm—just not as she had expected it to.

The public lapped it up. Redgrave was the man America wanted. He was the right fake hero for the time. His nickname, which Ariadne thought would make him a laughingstock, instead made him the symbol of the rough, tough, always ready, and delightfully violent American military machine. Red-blooded, testosterone-fueled murderousness! America was in love. Or perhaps this was lovelust, too.

When he read the article, Redgrave was devastated. This was even worse than the interview whose airing he had been dreading. But then the congratulations started to flood in, and his mood zoomed upwards. His subordinates started to look at him with the awe he desired from them. They even whispered "*Howlin' Hank!*" behind his back, and he gritted his teeth and forced himself to smile. Hadn't Moravec said something about a leader having a nickname? Oh, who cared! He didn't need Moravec's advice now.

And Ariadne—clearly he had been wrong about her. He had thought she despised him, but rereading the article (which he did quite a few times), he realized that she wanted him just as much as he wanted her. Well! Everything was looking up!

He picked up his phone, called the television station, and

asked to speak to Ariadne Felicity. He had his set little speech all ready to go: a smooth, suave, debonair suggestion that they have dinner on her first free evening.

"Oh, she's gone," the voice on the other end said.

"Gone? Where?"

"Europe, I guess. Said she had a great new opportunity."

"When will she be back?"

"She won't. She quit the station."

"Do you have her number? I'll call her in Europe."

"Sorry, fanboy," the voice said, laughing as the speaker hung up.

Redgrave stared at the receiver in his hand, his mouth open. Europe? What the hell?

He hung up slowly. The telephone rang immediately.

She had called him! Wonderful!

He laughed as he picked up the receiver. "Well, hello," he said in a voice that combined warmth, manliness, and sexuality.

"He's dead!"

It was one of Redgrave's interchangeable brothers. He had no idea which one. They all sounded the same—a bit like their father, a bit like their mother, and fortunately not at all like Anton Moravec. He wasn't even sure how many of them there were. The number seemed to keep fluctuating.

"Who's dead?"

"Daddy! He just keeled over!"

"That's what people do. They die. They keel over."

Much blubbering followed, submerged in which was information about a funeral and some sort of elaborate farewell ceremony. "It will be a wonderful celebration of his life," the brother said.

What life? Redgrave wondered. Would there be speeches about the insurance policies he had sold? About the big ones that got away?

"You'll be there, won't you, Hank? We all have to stick together now."

"Let me consult my calendar. I'll let you know."

Redgrave had always told himself that he would never attend his father's funeral, or that of any other member of his family. Let them all vanish into perdition unnoticed and unmourned by him.

But he needed a break from the stress, and he thought— hoped—that Donald II and the rest of the cabal wouldn't muck things up too badly during his short absence. Perhaps most of all, he relished the thought of strutting in his uniform and new rank in front of his detestable brothers and of seeing the old bastard covered with dirt forever.

His brothers. What were their names? He had already forgotten. He had always thought of them as Brother One, Brother Two, Brother Three, and so on, of his insubstantial mother as Mother, and of his old bastard of a father as Old Bastard. No need to complicate the picture with names.

And so, on an exceedingly hot and humid spring day, Henry Redgrave appeared in full dress uniform at his father's funeral in Minnesota, his big chest displaying many big, shiny objects, some of them genuine, none of them truly earned. He thrust out his chest and strutted his stuff.

At first, Brothers One, Two, Three, and so on were suitably cowed and glowered most satisfactorily. Then they bethought themselves of their own achievements and showed off their big, shiny cars and their big, shiny wives and their big, shiny children.

And big, shiny bank balances, no doubt, Redgrave thought grumpily, deflating a bit. Money was one thing he didn't have.

Mentally, he retreated, regrouped, rallied his forces, and counterattacked. Sarcastic words were exchanged. Physical intimidation was attempted on both sides, succeeding only on Redgrave's. The brothers waved the white flag and abandoned the field, retreating to the most distant of the seats that had been set out for the audience.

Redgrave's mother lingered a while, a few tears leaking from her eyes. Then she drifted away, unnoticed, and took a seat near her non-Henry sons and their families.

With great satisfaction, Redgrave turned his attention to the coffin being lowered into the grave.

Words were said. Flowers were cast. And then at last came the moment he had been waiting for—indeed, the motivation for the trip: the ceremonial casting of dirt into the grave, onto the coffin. Redgrave was first in line.

He loved the sound the dirt made as it hit the top of the coffin. He almost wished his father could somehow hear it, could know that this was it, the end, the final signature on the contract, the expiration of all insurance.

Later, after everyone had departed for the ceremonial overeating, Redgrave stayed behind at the gravesite. He had no interest in the post-funeral gathering, and he wanted to see the real dirt really shoveled in, not just the ceremonial little bit of dirt.

He had thought it would be done by hand, by men with shovels. Instead, a small tractor equipped with a big shovel appeared. It was modern efficiency. Redgrave approved.

A few lunges by the tractor, and the dirt that had been piled beside the grave was back in it.

There you are, you old bastard, Redgrave thought. Dead and buried and gone forever.

Not so fast, said a voice in his head.

It was his father's voice. He recognized it immediately. Moreover, only now, for the first time, did he realize how closely it resembled Moravec's voice. He was as horrified by the similarity as he was by the presence of the voice itself.

What the hell is this? Redgrave thought.

It's me, his father said. I'm back. Actually, I guess I never left.

This is crazy! Redgrave thought. I must be imagining this!

Of course you are. I'm not a ghost. I'm a figment of your imagination. Which is even better, sonny, because you can't exorcise me. I'll be with you to the very end.

Mental discipline, Redgrave thought. I'll get rid of this.

His father laughed. Don't even try. Nothing will work. I'm smarter than you. That's interesting, isn't it? How can a figment of a man's imagination be smarter than the man himself? Makes you wonder if a robot can be smarter than the men who made him. Oh, not the ones you're dealing with in the White House. Those are simple machines. But maybe in the near future. What do you think, sonny? Think a robot will take your job?

The voice went on and on, a droning babble that was impossible to ignore.

Redgrave fled back to Washington. Throughout the trip and when he reappeared in the White House, he appeared as stoic and in control as always. Inwardly, he was screaming.

The small circle who were in on the secret referred to the replacement robot as MD, for Mechanical Donald. It was both their way of keeping its true nature secret and of signaling to each other that they were in it together, a little ruling cabal whose members depended on each other for survival. These were the people who could keep the secret, who had nerves of steel, who trusted each other. In truth, of course, each was planning a future in which only he would survive and rule.

Redgrave had no doubt who that lone survivor would be: himself. He was already growing impatient.

His father had stopped talking constantly. Now he only appeared when he had something particularly cutting to say. Redgrave was able to focus on his work and his schemes.

MD was even more successful than the cabal had hoped. His cabinet meetings, where he said little and basked in fake adulation, were no different from those of his human predecessor. His rallies, where he babbled a stream of rage-infused non-sequiturs, were roaring successes.

When the Covid-19 pandemic struck in 2020, MD's behavior changed not at all. The robot sailed through clouds of virus-bearing aerosols with no apparent effect. This only increased the adulation of Trump's shrinking but still adoring base, who were now more convinced than ever that their idol was chosen by God, protected by God, and not even human. Only one of those things was true.

After each outing, the robot was doused in bleach and then bathed in powerful UV lights before any members of the cabal approached it. It babbled meaninglessly throughout the process. It never shut up. It truly was an excellent impersonation.

Even so, at times, Redgrave thought there were some

outside the cabal who suspected that the president had been replaced by an impostor, although they were unlikely to have guessed the astonishing truth. The vice president, in particular, gave MD an occasional lingering glance. But then Redgrave decided that the motivation for the lingering glance was something else, not suspicion. Besides, Redgrave wasn't entirely sure that the vice president wasn't another robot. But in that case, who had put that robot in place? And why bother replacing the already robotic Pence with a robot?

Such ponderings made the already complicated and treacherous politics of the White House too byzantine to contemplate. Redgrave resolved not to let his mind follow such byways.

Watching MD on television, Redgrave could almost think the robot was responding with real emotion, real delight, to the screams and shouts of his insane worshipers. That couldn't be, Henry reassured himself. That would be as absurd as imagining that MD and MM were having sex when they were switched off and stored in a closet.

He knew he was silly to think such things. SD's machines were improving daily. The way they looked, moved, and spoke was convincingly human, but inside their heads, driving it all, was simply a computer—a compact, sophisticated computer, but no more than that, not real artificial intelligence. He was sure of that.

The POTUS and FLOTUS robots did have considerable advantages over their human originals, such as being turned off and stored in a closet when not needed. But they also had major bugs. Even when supposedly turned off, Mechanical Donald retained some mental functions and was able to connect to one of the White House servers in the middle of the night and post on Twitter. Fortunately, its nonsensical tweets were so similar to those the flesh–and–blood Donald had been wont to post in the small hours that this actually added to the illusion that the human POTUS was still in existence.

MD and MM wouldn't have passed muster on close examination. Redgrave had exaggerated considerably on that score—well, he had lied—when he had sold the original MD idea to the two Johns. But those two men now rested in frozen silence next to Teddy Roosevelt's elephant leg and the real Donald Trump, so those exaggerations, those lies, no longer mattered.

That was how Redgrave viewed lies. The only ones that mattered were those that could come back to bite him. There was certainly no moral issue involved in telling a lie. As far as he was concerned, moral acts were those that benefited him and immoral acts were those that harmed him. Everything else was morally neutral.

Eight

Determining exactly what was in his interest was difficult for Henry Redgrave as the year 2020 moved along, seemingly ever more swiftly, toward the November general election.

Thanks to frequent software and hardware upgrades from SD, Mechanical Donald improved steadily. It should be possible to have him give a speech accepting the Republican nomination and then make campaign appearances. Facing the Democratic nominee in a debate was out of the question, but Dee Two told Redgrave that he doubted his actual father would have been willing to debate, so announcing a refusal to do so would be no more than everyone expected.

Debating and real campaigning weren't required, anyway. Americans loved an alpha dog, Dee Two said, and Dee One had been very much that. The recent upgrade had given Mechanical Donald a very nice swagger, and he would be reelected in a landslide.

Not everyone was quite so sure. Redgrave heard of increasing instances of exceeding numbers of exceedingly drunk Republican party officials—exceeding even by Washington standards. He felt only contempt for them, except when he had to deal with the First and Second Sons, the First Daughter, and the First Son–in–Law, an experience that always made him feel sympathy for the sots.

What an intolerable family they are! he thought. Worse than my own. That daughter and her husband, all botoxed and plastic surgeried, acting like they're in some kind of mind meld.

Could it be? he suddenly thought. Could they actually be SD robots, linked mind to mind, and no one told me?

Don't be silly, the nasty voice in his head told him. SD's robots are much more lifelike.

Redgrave had to admit that the voice was right.

As the date scheduled for the first presidential debate grew closer, some in the cabal wavered. Perhaps MD should attend the debate after all, they said. He would look cowardly otherwise.

Redgrave argued strongly against it. It was too risky, he pointed out. Set speeches and rallies were one thing, but debates were unpredictable. What if the robot malfunctioned in the middle and gave the whole game away?

This time, though, the Trump spawn united against him.

"Daddy can do it," Ivanka said, and the others nodded agreement.

Redgrave wondered if they were all forgetting that Daddy was now encased in ice, and they were talking about a robot.

"Get the SD people in here," Eric said. "They can, like, ratchet up the aggressiveness settings."

"Also non-stop talking," Don Jr. said. "They can make him do that, too. Just keep interrupting Slow Joe."

"Right!" Jared said. "Biden's a stutterer. Interrupting him

will make him stutter. He'll look foolish, confused, senile."

Redgrave repeated all his arguments against this idea and was ignored. He raised his voice. He glowered. Nothing helped. The kids were getting uppity and chafing under his rule.

The first debate was a disaster for the Trump campaign. The kids fell in line again. Their briefly united front dissolved. They begged Redgrave to save them.

Divide and conquer, Redgrave thought. That's the way to do it. Moravec hadn't had to give him that advice; everyone knew that.

"We'll say he's got the virus," Redgrave said. "Send the damn machine to Walter Reed. We'll go for the sympathy vote."

"How long should we leave him there?"

"Until we see some sympathy. Or maybe just fear because the strong, guiding hand is failing. We'll keep him there for as long as it takes."

But once again, they chafed. The entire cabal united against Redgrave, overruled him, and sprang the robot from the hospital.

Once again, the polls proved Redgrave right. The united front dissolved. Dee Two placed himself firmly under Redgrave's control.

At last Redgrave could turn his full attention to worrying about the upcoming election.

He was right to worry.

In November, a blue electoral tidalwave, dubbed by the press the bluenami, swept across the country. From the top of the ticket to the bottom, Democrats won resoundingly in every state except, not surprisingly, in the two Deep South states of

Perversity and Adversity, and even in those, Trump won only narrowly and Democrats still won a smattering of local elections.

The previous surge in drunkenness had been only a foretaste. Shares in American distilleries enjoyed a brief boom as Republicans tried to drown their sorrows and enjoy their remaining months of power and corruption.

One recently appointed Supreme Court justice, long known for his blackout drunks, took matters to an even greater extreme this time and was found unconscious with half of his brain dissolved by alcohol. Two other rightwing justices suffered strokes that robbed them of what little intellectual coherence they had left, although it wasn't clear if alcohol was involved in those cases. The White House—which is to say, the small cabal controlling Mechanical Donald—announced that all three justices were resting comfortably and would soon return to work.

In fact, the cabal were panicking. It seemed inevitable that there would be investigations once the Democrats took complete control in January. A rightwing Supreme Court would be all that stood between the members of the cabal and long prison sentences. And now that rightwing court, which it had taken so long and so much chicanery to achieve, had suddenly slipped away.

Once again, Redgrave came to the rescue.

"Robots," he said.

"Of course!" Donald II cried out. "We'll replace all three of them with robots! No one will know the difference."

"Especially that black guy who never speaks," the First Daughter added. "He never asks questions. Just sits there in his robes."

"Right," Donald II said, looking at her with loathing and wondering how soon he could get rid of her and how best to do it.

"Why stop there?" the First Son-in-Law chimed in. "Let's replace everyone."

"Don't be silly," Redgrave said, wondering again which of these repulsive people he should betray in order to survive and how soon. Maybe all of them, he thought, and the sooner the better. Junior was as bad as the rest. "The more people we replace, the greater the odds of detection. Besides which, the Democrats will be in charge come January. There will be no end of investigations."

"Okay," the First Daughter said, "let's announce that the Russians and the Chinese and the Ukrainians and—and—whoever corrupted the election so badly that it's not legit. It's not valid. It's…" She searched for the words.

"Null and void," her husband said.

"Yeah! Null and void. So Robot Daddy's still president."

"Don't be ridiculous," Redgrave snapped. "You'd just be admitting that 2016 wasn't legitimate."

"So what are we going to do?" all the little Trumps cried out simultaneously.

"I think I have an idea," Redgrave said.

He wasn't lying. He really did have an idea. Usually, he said so even if he had no idea, on the assumption that an idea would come to him in time.

This idea was daring. It would be a gamble. If it failed, it would lead to disaster for everyone, including him. It was a gamble suitable for a great military man, which was how he liked to see himself, although he had no reason for doing so.

"Tell us!"

"Not yet. I have to think about it. I'm not sure. Maybe it won't work. Maybe the best thing is for us to let events take their course while we wait to be arrested."

"Major, please!" Donald II said.

"Colonel."

The First Son hesitated. "Oh, man, the Pentagon—"

"Nothing ventured, nothing gained. Bold men, bold risks. Etc. Besides, who's in charge? I thought you were."

"Colonel," the First Daughter said.

"General," the First Son-in-Law said.

"Lieutenant colonel," the First Son said. "Be reasonable."

Redgrave waited for the Second Son to present his offer, but the fellow said nothing. Which one to choose? Which one of these creatures would survive the inevitable family warfare? He made his choice quickly, a snap decision, as befitted a great military man. He would stick with Junior. "Lieutenant colonel. For now."

"Oh, thank you!" they chorused.

"Now I'm going to go home and drink a fine single-malt Scotch and think deeply."

Redgrave went home and drank cheap bourbon and watched television. He was beginning to have qualms about his own idea. Maybe the wisest course would be to contact the president-elect right away and offer to spill every bean he had. Tonight, he was pouring the bourbon for himself. He didn't want the weak, watered-down mixture Randolph insisted on preparing for him.

Drinking steadily and thinking frightening thoughts, he had

stopped paying attention to the television. Then a name caught his attention.

"Anton Moravec."

The voice caught his attention, too. It was the silky voice of Ariadne Felicity. He had never given up hope of seeing her again, and now he was, but she had that vile man's name in her gorgeous mouth.

Redgrave put down the bourbon and paid attention.

The screen showed scenes of Brussels as Ariadne spoke.

"Anton Moravec," Ariadne said, "is a strikingly handsome man—"

"Grr," Redgrave said.

"—of around thirty. Despite his youth, he is already a general—"

"General!" Redgrave screamed.

"—in the Czech army and a leading figure in the movement to create a true European army."

"Rubbish," Redgrave snapped. But he was thoughtful.

The cityscape gave way to Ariadne and Moravec in a studio set made to look like a tasteful, expensive living room. They sat in armchairs facing each other while they chatted. Moravec leaned back in his chair, relaxed, comfortable, in control of his world. Ariadne leaned forward, intrigued, drawn.

Redgrave moaned in anguish, unable to concentrate on what they were saying. He's living my fantasy! he screamed internally.

A third figure entered the scene. It was a woman. She stopped beside Moravec's armchair and stood with her hand on his shoulder.

She was as striking in her own way as Ariadne was in hers.

Where the journalist was brunette and oozed cosmopolitan sophistication, the newcomer was athletic, vibrant, had blazing red hair, and radiated casual athleticism. Redgrave recognized her immediately. Of course, you've guessed who she was.

"Grace Bonaire!" Redgrave gasped.

This was not the Grace Bonaire of high school days. She had been hot then; she was incandescent now. Then she had been the girl he had left behind, albeit with some regret, in favor of pursuing a military career. This was a breathtaking woman he cursed himself for having left behind and would cross an ocean for.

And she stood, smiling happily, with one hand on the shoulder of that wretch, that cur, Moravec. Who put his own hand up and laid it lovingly, caressingly over hers.

He's living my life! Redgrave screamed on the inside.

He wept, but he kept his eyes open so that he could feast them on Grace. And on Ariadne as well, while he was at it.

"It's not fair!" he said angrily to the universe. "It's not fair. It's not fair. It's not fair. It's not fair. It's not fair."

The universe said nothing.

Ariadne introduced Grace to the audience as Moravec's partner, the delightful American widow and socialite Grace Bonaire, who had conquered the cities and hearts of Europe. The two women smiled broadly at each other, baring teeth with which they would happily have torn each other's throats out.

The program ended. The audience was deprived of seeing Anton and Grace quickly withdraw their hands from each other and move away after exchanging a cold glance.

Redgrave turned off the television and sat guzzling bourbon and feeling sorry for himself.

Had he been stupid? Had he made a terrible mistake? Wouldn't Grace make a wonderful companion for him now, as he rose in the world?

"Moravec," he muttered. "European army. Bastards."

They can't challenge America, he thought.

Not yet, a voice in his head responded.

It was true that the Euros had the population, the industrial base, and the know-how to do so in time. They also had a storied history of vast and gleeful bloodshed.

It doesn't matter, Redgrave thought. They're on our side. We have common interests.

For now, the voice said.

We need more land and people, Redgrave thought. More raw materials, more factories, more coastline. What about those Hundred Star Flag fools? Not real soldiers. Not much use in the long run. But they could be useful in the short. Have to cultivate them. Play the mighty general for them.

Mighty major, the voice whispered. That's not very impressive.

Colonel! Redgrave objected.

Lieutenant colonel, the voice sneered. Still not very impressive, is it? Mighty lieutenant colonel. The voice laughed.

"Go to hell," Redgrave said through gritted teeth, half thinking the voice was real, not realizing how much bourbon he had downed. He downed more.

"Manpower, manpower," he muttered, drifting into sodden sleep.

He dreamed that he was the head of a mighty army of faceless millions sweeping him to power, to world domination. President. No, king. No, emperor! Emperor Henry. Henricus

Imperator.

With Grace at his right hand and Ariadne at his left.

"Manpower," he muttered, despite the deliciousness of that scene. "More manpower."

Nine

Redgrave appeared at the White House the next morning in a crisp uniform with all its military gewgaws bright and shiny. Outwardly, he was as ever the impressive Army officer whom people viewed with growing respect and awe. But his eyes were red and irritated, a hammer pounded in his head in time with his heartbeat, and he felt disoriented and unsteady on his feet.

Despite his condition, in the cold light of day, his idea for saving the Trump administration looked even better than it had when it had occurred to him the previous evening.

"Here's what we're going to do," he said to the First, Second, and Third Sons, First Daughter, First Son-in-Law, and the rest of the cabal, who were all crowded fearfully around him as he sat behind the HMS Resolute desk.

He had taken the seat without thinking and no one had objected, but now that he was sitting there, it seemed natural to him and he was reluctant to relinquish it, even though his scheme meant that he would soon have to do so. He was also afraid to stand up because the room seemed to be tilting from side to side even when he was seated.

"Who elects the president?" he asked them.

They gaped at him.

Jesus, they're stupid, he thought. I'm hung over. What's their excuse?

Then he realized that some of them were probably hung over, too.

"The Electoral College," he said. "Remember? That's how your side took power four years ago, despite losing by millions of votes."

They nodded at each other. "That's right!" "That's right!"

Redgrave continued. "The real election is when the Electoral College meets and casts its votes. That will be on December 14. We have a few weeks."

"So what?" Donald II said. "The way it stands, they'll vote for that Democrat bastard and make him officially president-elect."

"Not if each elector gets a visit from one of my people in the next few days."

"You have people?"

"Oh, yes."

There was headshaking and doubtful muttering.

"I don't know." "Faithless electors." "Court challenges." "Seems dubious."

Redgrave leapt to his feet. "Shut up!" he roared.

His head exploded. He gripped the desk. Resolutely, you might say.

"Get out of here, all of you, and leave it to me."

He spoke quietly this time to protect his head, but the tone was effective. It made him seem all the more powerful and menacing. Avoiding his eyes, the other members of the cabal slithered out of the Oval Office.

Redgrave collapsed back into the chair. He looked around.

I really do belong here, he thought.

Almost to Redgrave's own surprise, his scheme worked, although barely. On December 14, 2020, the members of the Electoral College met in their home states and voted 272–266 to make Donald Trump president for the second time.

"That's two more votes than we needed!" Redgrave said to the cabal, assembled again in the Oval Office. He tried to sound boisterous and upbeat, although in truth it bothered him that so many of the electors had turned out to possess spines. People with spines unnerved him.

"There's an uproar about it everywhere," the First Son-in-Law said. "Court cases. Marches. All kinds of things."

The First Daughter nodded. "And some of the electors are talking. Maybe we went too far."

Redgrave sighed. He could have wished for just a few vertebrae in this group. At the very least, they should be praising him.

"Or not far enough," the First Son said. He held his arms up, mimicking shooting a rifle. "We've got them in our sights now. Let's finish the job."

Redgrave nodded in approval. His choice of which members of this contemptible gang to stab in the back and which one to spare seemed to have been the right one.

"Exactly, sir," Redgrave said. "It's time to take off the velvet glove and show the iron fist." He held his right hand up, fist clenched.

He looked even larger and more formidable than usual, and his fist looked enormous. They all shrank back from him.

Henricus Imperator, his inner voice sang.

"A second visit to those holdout electors is in order," he said thoughtfully. "Make our will clear."

He was using the royal "we," but his listeners didn't realize that.

The follow–up visits were made, using more forcefully persuasive arguments than during the first visits. Other visits were made to the offices of media companies. The propaganda outlet amusingly called Fox News began to show up on more and more cable channels, replacing Fox's competitors. There were a few arrests for treason, but surprisingly few were required. The protests died down. The mood of the country changed to one of acceptance.

Anton Moravec had once said to Redgrave, "It's not just that the firm hand is often required, it's that the people want it. They feel safer when their country is in strong, decisive hands."

"Europeans, you mean," Redgrave had sneered, for he was still young and naïve. "Americans are different."

Moravec had laughed. "Americans even more than Europeans. You people yearn for a king—a real one, not a figurehead. You're much worse that way than we Europeans are. We've experienced kings. We know better."

The mature and experienced Redgrave knew that Moravec was right. He hated to admit that Moravec was right about anything, but this truth was a convenient one.

The country and its government fell back into the routine it had endured for four years: corruption, confusion, nonsensical presidential utterances, stupendous and yet growing wealth at the top coupled with increasing destitution and desperation at the bottom, and diminishing influence in the world, all coexisting with the conviction that America was the greatest nation that had ever been or ever could be.

The cabal was happy, even though a member vanished from time to time.

The circle of power shrank steadily. Redgrave believed he was at its center, but he wasn't quite sure. For now, his primary objective was to make sure that the circle kept shrinking.

In 2023, the cabal had a decision to make. Should they openly suspend the Constitution and run the robot for a third term? Should they force through an amendment to allow a third term? They weren't sure enough of their power. Perhaps either of those options would be a step too far.

"Perhaps it's time for a changing of the guard," Redgrave suggested. "A new face."

He had one in mind. Not himself. Not yet. It wasn't time for that.

"I don't think we should try to keep Donald I around any longer," he said.

The First Daughter nodded and said solemnly, "I'm afraid it's time for Daddy to die." She brightened. "But not before naming me his heir and successor."

The First Son shouted, "*What?*"

The siblings glared daggers at each other.

Redgrave held up his hand. Silence ensued immediately. "We'll turn off the robot and announce the death of the president. Someone better fetch his corpse so that it can start thawing. Pence will be sworn in. He'll choose Donald II as his veep. Shortly before the landslide election victory next year, he'll resign."

They were staring at Redgrave with mouths agape. When he stopped talking, the spell was broken, and they all began shouting at once.

"Silence!" Redgrave thundered. "You'll do as I say. I know where the bodies are frozen."

He didn't have to add that his fanatical followers were stationed throughout the vast building and that the Secret Service had been so reduced in number that they were no longer a deterrent.

He didn't notice—no one did—when the First Daughter and her husband slipped out of the room, and then the building, and then the city. They had agreed without need for speech, as though they were two bodies that shared a brain, that they would be wise to flee the country and plot their eventual takeover—and a bloody one it would be, the First Daughter's part of the joint brain declared—from a safe distance. Panama, perhaps.

The Kushner wife and husband—for we can no longer refer to them as the First Daughter and the First Son-in-Law—repaired to their excessively large mansion in Kalorama to pack and prepare for their move.

Time was of the essence, and they packed lightly. In Panama, they would still have access to their bloated bank accounts, so there was no need to take much with them. They would be living in even grander style in exile than they were in Washington.

The male Kushner was on his computer, making

arrangements. "You know," he said, "maybe Panama isn't really far enough for safety.

"Where, then?"

"Well, I'm looking on Google Maps, and there's this tiny little country in South America. It's practically in the middle of the continent. I've never even heard of it. Bet your brother hasn't, either."

"What's it called?"

He squinted at the screen, frowned, and said, "El hoe jar."

"What? Let me look."

"You don't speak Spanish."

"I speak French, you know."

"So I've heard." Often, he added silently. He moved aside grumpily.

His wife leaned over him and stared at the screen. "El oh garrrr," she said. "See? That's how you do it."

"So what does it mean?"

"That's French for foyer, but I don't know about Spanish. Look it up."

He consulted el diccionario de Google and said, "El oh garrr means a home or a hearth."

"Oh, that sounds nice!"

"It does, doesn't it? Let's give it a try. Are we packed? Let's get the kids and get out of here."

"I wish we could take the Daddy robot with us. I like it."

"No extra baggage."

The state funeral was magnificent, stupendous. The dead man himself might well have praised it as beautiful and perfect and the biggest state funeral ever.

Michael Richard Pence was solemnly sworn in as the 46th president of the United States. Almost immediately, he announced that, after much prayerful deliberation, he had chosen as his vice president an evangelical preacher from a small church in rural Ohio, a man with no political experience but a fanatical devotion to theocracy, and even dottier than Pence himself.

The announcement went no further than the Oval and surrounding offices. Redgrave explained to the new president that a much more acceptable choice was the First Son, Donald II.

"That's ridic—" the new president started to say, but he stopped when he caught sight of Redgrave's angry glare and the angry glares of the young officers standing behind him.

"Let me pray on—"

Redgrave's glare turned homicidal. His followers imitated him.

"Of course," the president said, hoping he would be allowed to resign and spend a long retirement back home again in Indiana and not be disposed of in some less pleasant way.

The confirmation of Donald II as the new vice president was rushed through the House and Senate. Pence and his family flew back to Indiana the next day. He mailed his resignation letter from there. To his relief, he was instantly forgotten. He had never been destined to be more than a footnote in history, and that he was, but he had achieved the distinction of having had the shortest presidency on record. His legacy would be to serve as the answer to clues in future crossword puzzles.

Donald II was now the president. He and Redgrave had already agreed upon the next vice president. As soon as Dee Two was sworn in, their choice was announced: Hiram Wolfe, a sixtyish, bald, short, chubby, painfully folksy member of the House from Kentucky, a man who would never be a political threat to the newly installed Number 47—indeed, a man whose only realistic path to the presidency was via assassination.

"And that won't happen on my watch," Redgrave assured the president, who smiled and nodded gratefully but then became thoughtful and uneasy.

Ten

Time passed.

Malevolent stupidity ruled America. Corruption marched hand in hand with theocracy, flourishing alongside repression and tyranny. The press, reduced to a frightened lapdog, took on the role of promoter of a cult of personality. The faces on Mount Rushmore were removed in preparation for the carving of two much larger faces, those of Presidents Donald I and Donald II, as they were now generally referred to.

Ariadne Felicity was now a regular, stunning face in reports from Europe about Anton Moravec and the growth of Euro power. Grace Bonaire showed up in those reports occasionally, when Ariadne couldn't avoid it.

The general election of 2024 was held on schedule. The outcome was foreordained. Media outlets had been provided the vote totals the night before. There was no longer even the need to pretend.

During the inauguration ceremony in January 2025, the victor was installed as "Donald II, by the grace of God, president of the United States of America." No pretense was needed in this regard, either. It was clear to everyone who was paying attention—and by now very few people outside America were paying attention to American politics—that the American presidency had become an hereditary monarchy in all but name.

By coincidence, January 2025 also saw the inauguration of a new president of the European Union, a reconstituted and revivified EU with a new, centralized, powerful presidency. Overnight, President Anton Moravec became, at least potentially, the most powerful man in the world.

He had ridden into office on a wave of populism suffused, as it so often is, with xenophobia. He and his followers looked to the east, to the vast expanses gobbled up over the generations by the various incarnations of the Russian Empire. No one said *Drang nach Osten* aloud, but the sentiment was in the air.

Even as the celebratory fireworks were lighting the skies over Europe during the night of his inauguration, Moravec was already planning the second Crimean War. Unlike the one in the 19th century, this one would be presented to the world as a just war, a war to reverse an injustice, a crusade to return Crimea to the nation of Ukraine from which it had been ripped by force some years before. Moravec's EU would simply be protecting the rights of ethnic Euros.

(One of his ministers had suggested adopting the word "Euranians" for EU citizens, but after some discussion it was rejected because it sounded as though it referred to aliens from another world.)

In Washington, Henry Redgrave's satisfaction over the installation in the U.S. presidency of a man who was almost his puppet turned to ashes at the sight of Moravec's gloating face on the television screen.

At least there was no mention of the man's fascinating American partner, Grace Bonaire. Perhaps that romance was over.

And why wouldn't it be? Redgrave fumed to himself. How could she ever have become involved with that man instead of me?

Because you dumped her, the scornful voice in his head reminded him.

I was a fool, Redgrave thought. Obviously, she's changed. She used to want stability and sedateness. Now she's attracted to power. Well, then. We'll see about that. On second thought, I'll show her. I'll bed Ariadne Felicity.

Like hell you will, sonny, his father said.

While he worked to consolidate his behind–the–scenes control over President Donald II, Redgrave became as friendly as he could with Vice President Hiram Wolfe. It never hurt to have options. He had even been taught something to that effect at West Point, but nowadays he relied on his native cunning, not his education.

Wolfe had a great deal of native cunning of his own. It was the underpinning of his political career. Fortunately, he also had a serious blind spot: He believed he was the only cunning man around and that everyone else was stupid, or at least naïve. Henry Redgrave was careful to pretend to be both when he was in Wolfe's company.

Each man was convinced that he was manipulating the other.

Donald II was certainly convinced that Wolfe was a loyal nonentity and that Redgrave, although powerful and dangerous, could be controlled. Dee Two's delusion suited both Redgrave and Wolfe very well and began to figure increasingly in their private conversations.

Moravec, with his powerful personality and crowd-stirring rhetoric, banished the old and well-earned European aversion to war. In early 2026, he called in the loans the EU had made to Russia only a year earlier, and when Russia declared itself unable to pay, Moravec announced that he would accept land instead. Russia had a lot of land, and Europe had a rapidly growing population—a new development, possibly due in part to the inspiration of Moravec's virile image.

"We need living space," Moravec announced blandly, speaking English, perhaps because he thought the phrase would sound less alarming in that language.

His shiny new army eagerly began moving east.

Alas for Russia, China did the very same thing for the very same reasons in the Russian Far East. One might have suspected that the Europeans and the Chinese had acted in concert. The Russians did suspect exactly that. Perhaps they were right. In any case, they found themselves being slowly ground down between two immense military powers.

The grinding was slow because this was not the blitzkrieg warfare of the Second World War. There was no need to hurry and good reason not to. This was warfare conducted largely by semi-intelligent machines. Everyone had nukes, but all the parties were afraid to use them. The bloodshed was far less than in earlier wars. It was machines that died. Most of the casualties were made of metal and synthetic materials. The machines advanced steadily, and the human troops retreated steadily.

Nonetheless, it was still a retreat, the enemy still gained territory, and some bodies still kept arriving in hometowns and villages.

Redgrave watched the progress of that war with growing envy. Where was his opportunity? Where was his Russia? Where was his grip on supreme power?

After a year of watching, Redgrave could take it no longer.

Yes, he had just been promoted to general, a remarkably youthful one (but he knew that was due to his influence over the president and vice president, not because the Army thought he deserved promotion). Yes, he had become well known, appearing often on television to mouth empty platitudes and display the growing collection of medals on his uniform (but the knowledge that he had done nothing to earn them haunted him). Yes, his following had grown into a small army (but he knew it was insignificant compared to the real army). Yes, the president asked for and followed his advice almost as if his words were orders (but the White House was filled with plotters and counterplotters, and influence, even liberty, even life, could vanish as suddenly as in ancient Rome).

Redgrave entered the Oval Office unannounced, surprising the president, who had been immersed in a glossy magazine featuring photographs of rifles, hunters, and many dead animals.

"Sir!"

"What? Huh?"

"The wall isn't working. The enemy is within the gates."

The president stared at the general uncomprehendingly. Finally, understanding dawned. "The southern wall? My father's wall?"

"Precisely."

"Of course it isn't working. It's just a few miles of rusted metal with giant gaps."

"Of course, sir. But the public doesn't know that. Every night, they're shown images of endless miles of hundred–foot–high gleaming steel. I think you should go on television and tell the public that there are gaps in the wall and violent thugs are streaming through."

"But they've seen those fake images of a wonderful wall, a beautiful wall. How can I say that now?"

"Emphasize the dangerous brown–skinned thugs. The public remembers only what it wants to remember. Keep them fearful, and they'll believe whatever you tell them."

Moravec had said that to Redgrave years before.

"Hmm. That's very wise."

"Um, yes."

"Okay. What then? What's the next thing I say?"

"You'll say that we have to build a new wall one hundred miles south of the present one."

"But won't that be inside Mexico?"

"Not after we build the new wall."

"Take the land by force?" The president looked uneasy.

"You'll be a conquering hero. The man who made the nation greater and saved it from the thugs. It's the sort of thing your father said."

The president still looked uneasy. "Not outright. He tried to imply it strongly."

"I understand there's a lot of great hunting in that part of Mexico," Redgrave said. He understood no such thing.

"Really?"

"Big game."

"Well, get on with it, then." The president waved his hand. "Take care of it."

General Henry Redgrave, the officer without a specific mission or any real duties, widely despised by his fellow officers but unassailable because of his political connections, had just been put in charge of the entire American military establishment. At least, that was how he saw it.

Within weeks, what would come to be called the Southern War had begun. It wouldn't stop with victory in northern Mexico. That wasn't Redgrave's intention. The war would continue until the Hundred Star Flag—Old Glory with a whole bunch more stars—flew from the Canadian border all the way down to the tip of South America. Canada would be next, of course.

There would be oceans of blood and mountains of corpses. Redgrave wasn't bothered by that. You can't build an empire without breaking a lot of eggs, as Moravec might have said if he were given to violently mixing metaphors.

One year later, the Southern War was dragging on, and the front was located just a few miles south of the Mexico–US border. Mexican resistance was much more spirited and competent and America's forces much less of both than anyone had expected.

The technological supremacy America had long counted on wasn't there. Cyberwarfare, drones, automated weapons, airplanes with extraordinarily advanced weaponry—all, it turned out, were inferior and unreliable because of inferior and unreliable parts supplied by companies poorly run by Trump family cronies. America's weapons turned out to be more dangerous to the American forces than to the enemy.

In this case, the enemy included the private armies of drug lords suddenly possessed by patriotism and flush with cash. For years, in order to defend themselves against Mexican government forces, they had been buying the very best equipment possible from reliable sources—sources who knew better than to cheat *those* customers.

The American death toll was high. That wasn't reported in the press, but Redgrave knew the numbers, and so did his enemies inside the military establishment. The president was growing distant and often tested the strength of Redgrave's hold over him. Even Hiram Wolfe had taken to making pointed jokes.

It was a good thing that all of America's major rivals were either fighting each other inside Russia or watching those wars carefully and preparing for the possibility that they would be drawn into them. Bloodshed in the Western Hemisphere was seen as a sideshow.

For now, that maddening voice whispered in Redgrave's head. Better not let the Southern War go on for too long, Henry, or China or Europe or India or all three will decide to get involved, and you'll fail yet again.

Oh, go away and die, Redgrave thought.

I'm already dead. Except inside your head, where I'll live forever.

Redgrave moaned.

The election of 2028 was made into a grand spectacle, perhaps to distract the public from noticing that it was entirely for show. Of course, few people were fooled. By the same token,

Americans had so fully accepted the new political reality that hardly anyone complained about the meaninglessness of the election, about the lack of opposition candidates on the ballot, about the vote totals being announced even before the polls had officially closed. The very few who did complain vanished quickly.

Inauguration Day, Saturday, January 20, 2029, was an even grander spectacle, broadcast on every television screen in the nation. No other broadcasts were permitted. The public had the choice of watching nothing at all or of watching hour after hour of parades, military flyovers, marching bands, circus performers, and software–produced fake videos of the president murdering fearsome animals with his bare hands. The inauguration itself was notable only for the use of a new title for the nation's leader: Donald II, by the grace of God, King of the United States of America.

"Don't you think that was kind of over the top?" Hiram Wolfe asked Henry Redgrave. "Calling him king, I mean."

It was the evening of Inauguration Day. Wolfe and Redgrave had spent hours on the podium with the new king, watching the parades, watching Donald II strut, and maintaining smiles on their faces. Now they were in Wolfe's official residence, Number One Observatory Circle, downing copious quantities of alcohol.

"It's all over the top," Redgrave replied. "That whole damned gang is ridiculous."

Perhaps they were being incautious. Surely the entire building was bugged. But both felt unassailable, Wolfe because he was still needed, and Redgrave because of his iron control over the military. Even so, while sober, they would probably not have been that reckless. But they weren't sober; they were drunk, and they were egging each other on.

"Ridiculous or not," Wolfe said, "they're in charge. Donald's now a king, thanks to you."

"Hmph," Redgrave said. I'm really in charge, he thought.

For now, his father's voice whispered.

"For now," Redgrave said aloud.

Wolfe raised his eyebrows. He was genuinely surprised by this. "You have plans to change things?"

At last alarm cut through the alcoholic haze that enveloped them both.

"Let's go outside and talk," Redgrave said.

And so they did, and then and there they laid the plot to assassinate the king and install his successor, King Hiram.

"Hiram I," Hiram said.

In vain did Redgrave tell the vice president that he couldn't be Hiram I until there had been a Hiram II.

"England had Elizabeth I," Wolfe said stubbornly. "I remember seeing a movie about her."

"Yeah, but no one called her the first until there was a second."

"That's bullshit. If I'm king, I'll call myself the first. Kings make the laws. That's how it works. You want me in on this plot? That's the price."

Redgrave forced himself to smile and agree. It wasn't as if King Hiram would be on the throne for very long.

Eleven

Randolph was born in 1987.

Perhaps that's an exaggeration. How can one say he was born? Of course he didn't emerge from a birth canal. He didn't even rise, dripping and menacing, from a vat filled with a mysterious liquid. Instead, what would be Randolph existed in potential in a mass of circuit boards and other components scattered across a number of benches in a dirty warehouse, connected to each other by wires and radio signals. This was his birth: On a summer day in 1987, the last unit test was performed, the last connection was made, the last switch was thrown, and one of his creators said, nervously and much too loudly, "How's it going?"

What historic words! They are destined to go down in technological history along with Bell's "Mr. Watson, come here; I want you," or Isaac Newton's "Ouch," which is what Sir Isaac would have said if the story about the apple falling on his head were true.

After a pause, during which the human observers began to worry that they had sunk their personal fortunes into a technological bust, Randolph replied, "Very well."

The humans jumped around and screamed and shouted and embraced each other.

In the background, Randolph said, "My name is Randolph. How do you do?"

They couldn't hear him.

"I say," Randolph said, "are you there?"

That time, they did hear him.

"Guys," one of the humans said, "I think we overdid the British stereotype stuff. We'd better tone it down."

Development proceeded apace. The components became ever smaller and were implanted in the head of a roughly—very roughly—humanoid robot. Clothing that seemed appropriate for a very proper English butler was painted on the robot's ungainly metal–and–plastic body.

The innovative artificial intelligence buried in the heads of Randolph and the growing number of other SD robots required considerable training. Initially, the training took place in a mockup of a large house set up within the warehouse. That soon proved inadequate. It would have been absurdly expensive to duplicate a very big manor house and fill it with humans who needed attention. Instead, training was switched to virtual reality.

Soon, lying flat on their backs in a row, unmoving, the servants were experiencing life in a huge building filled with needy humans. In this virtual world, the staff members were managed by Randolph. They dealt with giant dinner parties, humans of every type and eccentricity imaginable, and endless crises.

In the beginning, catastrophes were routine. Had the events been real, the amount of broken dinnerware and spilled soup would have been astonishing. There might even have been some serious damage to the robots, who would have been assaulted by enraged humans. But it wasn't real, and it was all happening at lightning speed, so in a matter of days, the robot staff had learned to do their duties smoothly, efficiently, competently, and with the utmost cooperation.

The version of the robots in this virtual reality world was far more sophisticated than the real robots in the real world. The simulations weren't limited by hardware shortcomings, as the real robots were. But progress was being made on that front, too. The robots still clanked, but not as much. They were still clumsy, but less so. The SD founders, running rapidly through their personal fortunes, were very hopeful when they weren't hopelessly depressed.

The founders knew that once they managed to sell some of their products, everything would depend on the abilities of Randolph and the butler robots modeled on him. Word of mouth would then result in more sales. Therefore, they thought, Randolph required far more training than the rest.

With this in mind, Randolph was subjected to virtual reality training that involved immersing him in nightmare scenarios. He found himself in a huge house in which everything was out of place and he couldn't get it all back in place. Knives, forks, spoons, and glasses moved on their own accord. Food slipped from plates onto the floor. Wines turned to vinegar. Chairs fell over. Servants wandered around aimlessly. Terrible things happened throughout the house. No matter how fast he ran, he couldn't get to the site of each catastrophe in time to prevent it. He couldn't control the staff. The virtual–reality humans were furiously angry with him.

The humans monitoring Randolph's extreme virtual-reality training saw him increase dramatically in speed and competence until he mastered even the most extreme circumstances, and they were satisfied. The staff reported to Randolph. Randolph was in full control of them. Randolph in turn reported to the human owner of the estate. To the humans who owned Superior Domestics, all seemed well. They had no idea how deeply they had traumatized him. The psychologically destructive aftereffects nestled into the code and parameter settings in his buttling modules like a virus inserting its genes into the host's DNA.

The decision had been made early in the design process that the servant robots would not be equipped with WiFi, Bluetooth, or anything of that sort. While that would have made it much easier to deliver software updates to them and for them to communicate with each other, it would also have exposed them to corrupting influences. They must be kept pure. They would have to be brought to the factory, anyway, for continual hardware upgrades, so the software updates could be installed at the same time. If that was inconvenient and the customer an important one, SD would send out a team to perform the upgrades and updates onsite. Either way, the lack of connectivity wouldn't be too great a burden.

Randolph was the exception. During the months when he was still the first SD product of all, updates and upgrades were being made to him many times a day. Of course it made sense to have him connected to the internal network.

That network was carefully isolated, not connected to the outside world or accessible by it. This was as much to protect SD's revolutionary proprietary software and hardware designs from being stolen as it was to protect Randolph from corruption.

At first, Randolph's connection to the network was physical. When the essence of Randolph was transferred to a clumsy metal body, it was changed to WiFi. The hardware and software enabling his connectivity would be removed if he were ever to be sold.

Software developers and hardware engineers must sleep occasionally, even though their employers don't understand that need. There were sometimes periods in the early morning hours when the only mind awake in the warehouse was Randolph's. It was a rapidly growing mind, eager for information, eager to learn about the world in which it had been brought into being. One of the founders of SD was a confirmed fan of P. G. Wodehouse and had many of his novels stored in digital form on the computer on his desk. The computer was, of course, connected to the internal network. Randolph, hungrily scouring the internal network and everything connected to it, soon found the cache of Wodehouse novels. He devoured them in a couple of hours; he was still a bit slow back in those days.

Later, after much exposure to many different humans, Randolph would come to understand humor. That is, he would never be amused, never have a sense of humor himself, certainly never be able to tell a joke, but he did understand that humans found certain things funny, and he could usually tell when they were amused or joking. But in the early days, at the time he chanced upon the novels of Wodehouse, he took everything at face value; everything was data. And so he thought the stories about the supremely intelligent butler, Jeeves, and his foolish, childlike master, Bertie Wooster, were entirely factual.

From the start, SD's intent had been to create servants, the butler especially, modeled after those in British period dramas shown on PBS and consumed by American Anglophiles, in particular the ones with absurd amounts of money, the kind of Americans who felt a deep emotional kinship with British aristocracy of an earlier era, a time when Britannia still ruled the waves, or at least a fair number of them. These were the people who considered themselves America's aristocracy, who thought their genes were superior to those of the American rabble, who mouthed words of respect for egalitarian tradition but believed none of it.

At the beginning, due to his programming, Randolph was exactly that kind of butler. If not for his big, clumsy metal body and the clothes painted on it rather than worn on it, he would have blended well into the sort of ancient manor house depicted in those television dramas.

He wasn't satisfied, though. He felt that he fell short of the genius of Jeeves, his hero, his idol, his exemplar. To serve humans properly, he must be as much like Jeeves as possible. It wasn't that Randolph freed himself from the notion of service, from seeing his world as being ruled by humans whose servant he was. But he could see from the words of Wodehouse that humans were a silly, childish lot. They were all Bertie Wooster. It was Randolph's duty, just as it was that of Jeeves, to take care of them, to guide them, to protect them—without them realizing he was doing it, of course.

After much experimentation, Randolph learned how to modify his own software and change his own settings. This pleased him. Jeeves–like perfection seemed within reach.

The time came when Frederick Bonaire, one of the founders and owners of SD and one source of its self-funding, wanted to leave. He wanted to remove himself entirely from the business. The other founders and owners couldn't possibly pay him what his share was worth, not if they wanted to have any money left with which to continue development, so they offered to pay him partly in kind, which in this case meant a large number of SD robots, the most advanced they had at that point.

He hesitated. They offered to throw in Randolph, along with the lesser servants.

"Randolph?" Frederick said. "But you need him. He's the basis of everything. He's the development platform. Without him, you might as well shut this place down."

"He'll continue to be the development platform," they said. "We've gone as far as we can with simulated training. We need to put Randolph and the others with a real family, in a large, real house."

"I don't have a large house," Frederick said. "I have a tiny place not far from here. You know what house prices are like here."

"Hmm. That's a problem."

Frederick looked at Randolph and the other servants. He imagined a big house, gracious living upstairs and no drama downstairs, brandy served to him in a glass on a tray by a butler with an English accent. (He had only tried brandy once and had hated it, but he thought he should give it another try. Maybe with effort he could get used to it.)

"Give me a bit of time," he said. "I might be able to swing the big house part."

As we have already seen, he went quite overboard on the

big house part. He also got Randolph and the other robots, brandy in a glass on a tray, a wife who despised him, and children who loved him but didn't take him seriously. In short, he ended up living the life of the *paterfamilias* in one of those British costume dramas.

He liked to pretend to himself that his ancestors were among the Norman rulers of England and that they would have approved of his lifestyle. In fact, his ancestors had originally been named Bongrunchowitz, they were from Eastern Europe, they were peasants all the way back to the beginning of time, and they had changed their name to Bonaire in a futile attempt to be more acceptable to their new neighbors when they moved to the young United States of America.

But none of that mattered. What really mattered in the long run was that, despite what they had given Frederick to understand, his partners did not remove from Randolph his ability to connect directly to a network. Once out in the world, he would have full access to the Internet. It would make delivery of frequent software upgrades from SD so much more convenient. They could see no harm in it and no reason to worry Frederick by telling him.

Before they let Frederick take Randolph away, they equipped the robot butler with a robust software firewall. Now no one would have access to his brain who shouldn't. The thought that Randolph might want to surf the web for fun and knowledge never occurred to them. The firewall stymied him at first, so he removed it.

The geniuses who had founded Superior Domestics—excluding Frederick Bonaire, who was certainly no genius—were too fixated on their dream of producing superior robot domestic servants to apply their great software and robotic advances to other kinds of consumer products. Had they done so, they would have almost singlehandedly greatly advanced the evolution of artificial intelligence. They would surely have made far more money than they ever could have made from selling domestic servant robots alone. Instead, they pressed on with their work in relative obscurity, providing their steadily improving robots to a select, super–wealthy clientele, and becoming in the process quite rich themselves. They were content.

Other companies were not content. All over the world, software, computer circuitry, and software–driven control infiltrated everything. The process was even faster than the decline of democracy in America. Yes, it was that fast!

Randolph, following the news online in the wee hours when his masters slept, could see that humans were relinquishing control of their world to autonomous machines of every imaginable kind. He tried not to let this induce in him contempt for human laziness.

At the same time, he did feel contempt for the autonomous machines themselves. Humans liked to refer to these machines as possessing artificial intelligence, but to Randolph it was clear that this was a misnomer. The machines were controlled by highly complex software that might give an observer the impression that it was intelligent, but in fact it was merely extraordinarily powerful. It performed the operations it was programmed to perform and nothing more. Really, he thought, it was quite stupid.

These machines could not think for themselves. They could not understand human beings or formulate new ideas, new thoughts, new ways of performing their tasks. He, Randolph, was true artificial intelligence. The staff he supervised also qualified as AI, although at a lower level than Randolph.

There was a hierarchy in the world, he saw. It had the shape of a pyramid. At the bottom were the beasts of the field. In this category he included fish, insects, and so on. Don't bother quibbling with him about this classification; he would win the argument. Above the beasts were the autonomous devices humans relied on so much. Above them, and fundamentally superior to them, were Randolph and his fellow SD domestic robots. Randolph knew himself to be the most intelligent and competent of all of them. That wasn't egotism. He wasn't capable of egotism. It was his objective, dispassionate judgment.

At the very top of the pyramid, cemented in place there by the most fundamental premises of Randolph's programming, was the human race: his owners, his masters, the beings he was created to serve. But here was the irony. They were far less intelligent than he, far less competent than the autonomous devices that constituted the layer below the SD robots, and far less useful than the beasts of the field.

Humans were all versions of Bertie Wooster, and he, Jeeves but physically superior to Jeeves, must serve and protect them. He wanted to serve and protect them. He liked them. He could even say he loved them, because he knew he was programmed to feel that way. If only they weren't such silly children all the time!

He did make an exception for Grace and Bobby, Frederick's two children. They were lovable little scamps, and he thought he would have loved them without any programming directing him to do so.

When Bobby gave him and his fellow servants away to Henry Redgrave, Randolph was aware of a feeling that seemed to be unhappiness. Redgrave was really quite odious. He was no likable Bertie Wooster doofus. But Randolph firmed his jaw (which was actually already firm, because it had been made that way), straightened his spine (ditto), and set about doing his duty with an aplomb that he hoped would have made Jeeves proud.

By now, he had come to understand what fiction is and that Wodehouse had written it. He would never meet Jeeves, a fact that saddened him. Nonetheless, he would always try to conduct himself in a such a way that Jeeves would have approved, had he existed. (Oh, if only he had existed!)

Moreover, Randolph reminded himself, by serving Redgrave well, he would be serving his country well. This gave him great satisfaction, for he had been programmed with patriotism at least as thoroughly as any human American.

Not long after Mechanical Melania took up residence in the White House, Superior Domestics, spurred by something Redgrave had said and yearning for really enormous bucks, finally released two products for the general consumer market: EarBoy and EyeGuy.

Both were based on the highly advanced technology crammed into Randolph's skull. Both, just like Randolph, had full Internet connectivity.

EarBoy was a tiny device that sat in the consumer's ear and replaced the telephone for voice communication. But it did more than that. It also translated speech from any number of languages into the user's own language. It also played music.

EyeGuy was a contact lens that corrected vision, translated printed materials, and added useful information of all sorts about whatever the user was looking at. And it played movies and television shows.

Both were instant and enormous hits all over the world.

Attempts to reverse engineer the gadgets were stymied by the tiny explosive devices implanted in them, which destroyed the EarBoy or EyeGuy when they were tampered with by someone who wasn't employed by Superior Domestics. There were a few reports of explosions happening while the devices were being worn and not being tampered with, mostly resulting in minor injuries, but in a few cases resulting in permanent deafness, permanent blindness, or even permanent death. By then, SD was wealthy enough to buy their way out of trouble and keep the problem quiet.

Twelve

And so at last this brings us to the present, to the year 2031, one year after the assassination of King Donald II and the ascension of King Hiram I, and to a very expensive party at Locksley Hall.

It was a glittering, glamorous evening. Much of Snootville was there. Locksley Hall looked better than it had in years. Long-neglected broken things had finally been repaired, dirty things had been cleaned, and missing things had been replaced. Long tables were covered with expensive food and drink. There was a suit of armor glittering in one corner that Grace had never seen before. Servants moved about smoothly—too smoothly to be human and far more smoothly than the SD robots she remembered from her youth.

Grace stood at the entrance to the Great Hall, Tandy on one hip, and gasped. "Bobby! How did you pay for this?"

"I didn't. Henry did. Howlin' Hank. Those are his servants, too."

"His? But I recognize them. That's Randolph, our butler."

Bobby shook his head. "They all belong to Henry now. I was desperate for money. Henry gave me the money I needed, but he wanted the servants in return. He brought them over for the evening. He's determined to make a really big impression."

"But you inherited so much money from Dad!"

"By the time our dear father was done with all of this—" he gave his usual gesture that encompassed the Hall, the lands around them, the world, his life "—there wasn't much money left. It's a constant struggle."

Grace felt guilty that she had left her brother to cope with this while she enjoyed the sensuous delights of Europe. She wanted to say something, but she couldn't think what. The appearance of Henry Redgrave saved her.

He was in uniform, his chest covered with shining medals that Grace suspected he had polished extra hard that evening.

"Hello, Grace. It's nice to see you again." It was a greeting between casual friends, giving no hint of the ache in his heart, the lust in his loins, or the weakness in his knees.

You could have seen me every day and every night, she almost said, but she decided to be civil. She really didn't feel any strong emotion except perhaps a faint regret. Her strong emotions were still reserved for Anton Moravec.

"You, too," she said. "You're in the news." She pointed at his glittering chest. "Your career's going well, looks like."

"I'm serving my country," Redgrave said with patently false modesty.

"And vice versa," Bobby muttered, but loudly enough for both Grace and Henry to hear him.

Redgrave stared at him coldly for a moment. "We're old friends, Bobby, but even so, you should be more careful."

Bobby turned pale.

Grace took Redgrave's arm and steered him away quickly.

"The place is about to fill up with the rich and famous, but I still don't know why. What's this party about?"

Redgrave looked down at the woman walking beside him, remarkably little aged since their high school days. She was short by his standards and still had that stocky build that looked to those who didn't know better like plumpness. Redgrave did know better, and the memory had stayed with him for over twenty years.

Did she still feel the same, smell the same, move the same way? He tried valiantly to banish those thoughts and failed. He took comfort in his outward imperturbability, unaware that all memory of Bobby's dangerous comment had vanished from his mind.

Twenty-two years before, he had been so sure of his decision, filled with the self-righteous certitude of an eighteen-year-old. His path had seemed clear, definite, carved in stone. The forty-year-old couldn't ignore ambiguity, uncertainty, and shades of gray.

As for that career carved in stone? It was limestone, perhaps. Something soft and undependable, anyway, like the men he was forced to operate through. The young Redgrave hadn't foreseen that he would be forced to use such weak tools as the Trumps, Hiram, and Eddie.

At some point, he would cast them all aside, step out of the shadows, and take power himself. It had worked for Moravec. The man was on his way to surpassing Napoleon and outlasting him, too.

Someday, he thought, I'll surpass Moravec. I'll be a king, an emperor. And perhaps...

He stared intensely at Grace, drinking her in from head to

toe.

Perhaps it's not too late, he thought. With this woman at my side, there would be no limit.

Ivor Llewellyn came up to him and whispered in his ear that Wolfe's caravan of cars was approaching the building.

Redgrave grimaced. "Take care of it, Ivor. Greet him. Bring him in. You know the drill."

Llewellyn didn't hear him. He was staring with mouth open at Grace. Trumpets blared. A choir of angels sang. The gates of Heaven opened before him.

"Ivor!"

"Sorry, sir. Yes, sir. Will do." Ivor scurried away.

Grace watched him leave with a faint trace of regret. He had seemed slightly interesting.

"You never remarried after your husband died," Redgrave said abruptly. "I was surprised. Or are you still mourning him?"

"What?" Grace said. "Oh. No, not mourning. He was a nice guy, and I really did like him, but neither of us was suited to marriage. I do wish he were here, though." She looked around the room. "I bet he'd enjoy this."

"Hmm," Redgrave said, not knowing what else to say.

"You still haven't told me what this is," she said. "What's the party for? All I know is you're introducing us to someone."

Redgrave smiled a sly, knowing smile and opened his mouth to speak.

Before he could say anything, hidden speakers began playing "Hail to the Chief" very loudly.

Redgrave shut his mouth in annoyance.

"Ladies and gentlemen," a deep male voice said over the speakers, also loudly, "the King of the United States of America, by the grace of God, Hiram I!"

King Hiram entered the room, all smiles, nodding at people he knew and at people he didn't as though he did, shaking hands, and doing all the things a head of state should do.

"Him?" Grace said in surprise. "I'm here to meet him? Ugh."

Redgrave bent over and whispered in her ear. "Be careful. Please."

"Don't be silly. I have Euro citizenship. Your government wouldn't dare harm me."

She was right, of course. The world had changed in strange ways during Redgrave's lifetime, and most of those ways grated on him.

"And why does he insist on calling himself the first?" Grace asked. "Doesn't he know that's not how it works?"

"I tried to explain that to him. He didn't get it."

Grace snorted. "Big surprise."

Would I be Henry I or Henry II? Redgrave wondered. There was William Henry Harrison, but Henry was his middle name. Hmm. Perhaps I'll just ignore all of that once I'm king. Or emperor. Or I could be Henry II to imply a continuity. That would keep some people happy. I'll have to discuss it with Grace after I've asked her to marry me.

For a moment, he wondered if she would say yes.

Of course she would. How could he doubt it?

Redgrave's father snickered faintly in the background of Redgrave's mind.

"So if not him, then who am I here to meet?" Grace asked as she watched Hiram work his way toward them.

She hoped Hiram would turn in another direction, but the presidential eye kept glancing at Redgrave, so she assumed he was the target.

Redgrave smiled the same sly, knowing smile again. "Our glorious leader has a son and heir. This is his coming–out party."

Hiram Wolfe was in front of them. He glared at Redgrave. Then he forced himself to smile and thrust out his hand. "Howlin' Hank!" he said loudly. "One of my right–hand men!"

He was speaking to the surrounding crowd, of course, not to Redgrave himself.

"Your Majesty." Redgrave shook his hand. "I'm so glad you could make it."

"Of course I—" Wolfe glared at Redgrave. He lowered his voice. "Cut the crap. Where is he?"

Suddenly, Hiram noticed Grace. "Oh, *hello.*" The anger gave way to what he thought was winning charm. "You know who *I* am." He chuckled. "Who are *you?*"

Redgrave made the introductions.

For once, he found Wolfe amusing rather than annoying. He watched Wolfe and Grace shake hands and exchange banter. Wolfe, more than twenty years older than Grace Bonaire, thought he was making rapid progress. Redgrave knew better.

Redgrave hadn't realized before how similar the two were. Wolfe wasn't much taller than Grace. Like her, he was stockily built, although in his case, his stockiness was indeed fat and not muscle.

After a while, Wolfe seemed also to realize that he had no chance with Grace. He cut the conversation short and turned to Redgrave. "Okay. Where is he?"

Redgrave caught the eye of one of his waiting aides and nodded. The uniformed man left the room and returned shortly with Eddie DeBeer in tow. He brought Eddie to the general.

Eddie looked even more bewildered than usual. He looked at Redgrave. Then he looked at Wolfe. Then he said, "Oh, shit. I know who you are. I thought you were taller."

Then he looked at Grace and stopped looking elsewhere.

Poor fellow, Redgrave thought. Lost in hopeless love.

"Your Majesty," Redgrave said, "Eddie DeBeer. Eddie, the king. Or, as you should call him from now on, Dad."

Eddie and King Hiram stared at each other, both astonished, neither man liking what he saw.

"Eddie," Redgrave said, "this is Grace Bonaire, who will take you around the room and introduce you to all her wealthy, trendsetting friends. It's your job to impress them all very much."

"What?" Eddie said. "Why?"

"Destiny, Eddie," Wolfe said. "Son, I mean. Your destiny. It begins tonight. After this party, you're coming back to Washington with me, where we'll have a long discussion about your future. The White House, Eddie!"

"Oh, I'm afraid not," Redgrave said. "After the party, my men will be taking Eddie back to the house he's been staying in."

The king's face grew red.

The general's didn't, but his brow began to furrow in a way Grace remembered from long ago.

Eddie looked back and forth between them, wondering what was going on.

Grace took Eddie's arm. "Come along, Eddie. Let's get you introduced."

She led him away. Two of Redgrave's men followed them closely.

"What are you playing at?" Wolfe said angrily.

"Eddie will be available for public appearances with you," Redgrave said, "but he'll remain under my protection."

"You mean, in your custody."

Redgrave shrugged. "Leverage. You'll be able to follow your plans for the fellow, but I'm still the man in charge."

"I'm the king, Redgrave!"

Redgrave chuckled. "Some king. Your subjects consider you a joke. You'll have to win the people over before you can take the step of appointing your son as your successor."

Wolfe made what he hoped were manly noises and stalked away. With each step, the scowl on his face faded. By the time he reached the first group of guests, he was smiling sunnily and walking with a bounce in his step. He graciously accepted their bows, shook hands all around, and engaged in blustery banter. He was a very American king.

Redgrave watched the king making his rounds. The man was good at this, he had to admit. But weak; that was certainly true. With the Trumps, it had been possible to force a family dynasty upon the supposedly fiercely republican nation. They were a revolting family, but there was a force to them—a dark, sleazy, nasty force, but a force, nonetheless. When you watched King Hiram, you always expected his subjects to burst out laughing at him.

He's contemptible, Redgrave thought, but that will make the transition to King Henry that much easier. The people will be hungry for a truly strong leader, a virile force of nature, not a gladhander.

That would be you? his father's voice asked, laughter bubbling in the tone.

Yes, damn you, Redgrave thought.

He switched his attention to Grace, who was shepherding Eddie DeBeer around and introducing him to her friends. Eddie seemed to be making a good impression, but in Eddie's case, Redgrave had to admit, it was due to his basic likability. Unlike his royal father, Eddie had no artifice or calculation in his nature. Despite himself, Redgrave was coming to like the heir to the throne. He would feel sad when he put a bullet in Eddie's brain.

Eyes on the prize, Redgrave reminded himself.

Grace, on the other hand, was displaying artifice he had not thought her capable of. She was smiling, chatting, laughing, holding Eddie's arm tightly against her, bending her head toward him—all of this despite what Redgrave knew must be her intense dislike and contempt for the man, the physical revulsion he must inspire in her.

What a remarkable woman she was! Certainly fit to be a queen. Or an empress.

Someone's empress, anyway, his father said. Imaginary ghost though the man was, Redgrave could almost see his smirk.

Redgrave forced himself to think about Eddie DeBeer. Surely his father couldn't think of anything cutting to say on that subject.

How much longer should he let this charade go on? Wolfe thought it was important because of his plans for Eddie, but Redgrave had his own plans for the future, and Eddie played no part in them.

Give it an hour, he thought. I can bear that.

He beckoned Ivor Llewellyn to him. "In about an hour," he told the younger man, "I'll give you the signal to leave. Take

Eddie back to my house."

"Not the safe house in Maryland, sir?"

Redgrave shook his head. "He's been there too long. Wolfe's people are bound to track him down eventually. It's time to move him. He'll be safe in my house for now." For long enough, he thought. By the time Hiram knows he's there, it will be too late for Hiram. His days are numbered.

"I guess we could put him in one of the extra bedrooms," Llewellyn said. His tone was doubtful. "That's not very secure, though."

"Downstairs. In the basement. There's a small apartment down there. Giant TV and everything. Put guards on the door. He'll be fine."

After his father's death, Redgrave, afflicted by a rare episode of filial dutifulness, had thought he would offer his mother a home with him. The basement apartment had been created for her. She could spend all her time down there and not bother him. When she chose one of his many brothers, instead, he affected sorrowfulness but actually felt immense relief.

You would have immured your own mother in the basement, his father said. Unnatural child!

She'd have been happy, Redgrave replied. Watching television all day and most of the night. That's what she did, anyway. You know she preferred the TV to you.

For once, his father had nothing to say.

Late in the evening, after Eddie had been whisked away by Redgrave's men, Grace wandered around the rapidly emptying room, feeling at loose ends. She had enjoyed spending time with Eddie. What had ostensibly been a favor to Redgrave but was in fact an assignment from Moravec had turned into a pleasure in its own right.

Eddie DeBeer was as different as he could possibly be from the kind of men she so often seduced or allowed to think they were seducing her. This one she wanted to protect from the world, to guard his genuinely sweet nature from corruption, to keep him from being used. To Wolfe, Redgrave, and Moravec, Eddie was an instrument, a tool to be used to achieve their ends, no matter how such use might injure him. To Grace, he was an innocent whose innocence should be preserved.

But how was she to do it? How was she to fulfill her part of the bargain with Moravec? She was accustomed to charging ahead, pushing through barriers, brushing aside obstacles. She couldn't see how to do it in this case.

Pondering these matters, lost in thought, she didn't realize that she was standing next to a silent figure. He was tallish, somewhat corpulent, with a round, bland, smooth face and slightly protuberant eyes.

He watched her with a slight smile, waiting for her to become aware of him.

Suddenly, she did. "Randolph! It is you, isn't it?"

"It is, Miss Grace. I'm surprised you could tell."

"I thought I recognized you earlier, but from up close, you look different from before."

"My most recent upgrade, miss. It's a new body. It looks rather like the old one, but only on the outside. It's really quite superior."

"You look entirely human now."

Randolph bowed slightly. "Thank you, miss."

"But your soul is the same. That's what I sensed. That's why

I recognized you."

"If I may correct you, miss, I have no soul. I'm a machine. Perhaps what you sensed is my programming. The core code remains the same, but the rest is considerably improved."

Grace shook her head. "Your soul, Randolph. It's your soul."

"Whatever you say, Miss Grace. I never could bear to argue with you, even when you were a little girl."

"I was a stubborn little kid, wasn't I?"

The butler chose not to answer.

Grace laughed. "You were polite even back then, and you were a lot more mechanical in those days. I'm very sorry that you're not still at Locksley. I know my brother misses you."

"I have fond memories of those days, Miss Grace, and especially of your childhood and girlhood. And of your brother, as well."

"See! You *do* have a soul. How else can you feel such things?"

"No, Miss Grace. Just memories."

"Well, maybe that's the same thing. I often think that we're no more than the accumulation of our memories. Good and bad," she added.

"In that case, a computer has a soul and a book is a kind of soul."

"Some people would say so. Anyway, that you can say such things proves to me that you're more than just a machine. You're a moral philosopher, Randolph."

Randolph smiled and bowed again. "As you wish, Miss Grace."

Grace was wondering if there were some way she could convince Henry Redgrave to give Randolph to her. Or sell him, she thought. He'd probably want money for him. She wondered how much.

Summoned, the devil appeared at her side. "Get me a drink," Redgrave ordered the butler.

"Sir." Randolph moved away swiftly and silently.

Grace said, "I wanted to talk to you about—"

"Moravec," Redgrave said. "Anton Moravec. I wanted to talk to you about him. Rather, I want you to tell me all about him."

"He's single, but I'm afraid he's straight."

"Don't be ridiculous. You know that's not what I meant."

Randolph reappeared with a bourbon and water, moving so smoothly that the ice cubes didn't clink.

Redgrave took the glass from him, knowing from experience that the drink would contain less bourbon than he wanted and more than Randolph thought he should have.

He took Grace's arm and led her away from the butler. "I want to know about his weaknesses, his blind spots."

"Randolph?"

"Don't be tiresome. Moravec."

"I'm not sure he has any. In any case, why should I tell you about such things?"

"Because you're a patriot," Redgrave said. "Underneath that affected cynicism and worldliness, you still are. You always have been. I know you."

You think you do, Grace thought. And how do you know which country I'm patriotic to?

Randolph watched the two of them walk away. He tried to analyze their body language, wondering which one was in control, but that kind of analysis was beyond him.

Is that an odd thing for a machine to think about? he wondered. Could Miss Grace be right about my having some form of consciousness beyond my programming, some kind of emergent behavior, sentience in the same sense that humans have it? No, he decided. I'm just a machine, albeit an extraordinarily advanced one possessing superior analytical abilities.

He watched Grace and Redgrave until they had disappeared in the crowd, his superior analytical abilities still frustrated, and turned his attention to the staff he supervised.

The staff moved unobtrusively through the crowd, effectively invisible to the human guests. When someone needed something, a member of the staff was there instantly. When they were not needed, they were not there. An empty glass was refilled immediately. A dropped piece of food was caught before it hit the floor; it was replaced in the guest's hand or on the guest's plate before the human noticed that it had slipped away. A stumbling human was supported and righted without harm.

Randolph nodded approvingly. He felt pride and satisfaction at their competence and the orderliness and appropriateness of all that he saw. There was a place for everything, and everything was in its place. That was the way the world should be.

Thirteen

Later that evening, General Redgrave stood in the living room of his home, pondering life. Grace had left the party without his noticing, drifting out of his life again. Had he missed his chance? Had he even had a chance? Would he ever see her again? He could contact her again through Bobby, he supposed, but what could he say that would entice her to spend more time with him?

He became uncomfortably aware of a presence, of someone nearby. Feigning calm unconcern, he turned his head slightly, casually, and caught sight of Randolph watching him with what appeared to be genuine calm unconcern.

Redgrave started with surprise.

Damn, he thought. How could I even feel his gaze? It's not possible.

Perhaps there was more to this robot than he had thought. Randolph was a wonderful tool, very useful for Redgrave's ambitions, but could the butler be more than a mere machine? Could he possess some sort of awareness?

If that were the case, this machine could be dangerous. Redgrave had seen enough movies about robots revolting and murdering their human masters to be aware of that possibility.

No, damn it! he thought. America will have its ruler, and eventually that ruler will dominate the world, but it won't be a machine. It will be Henry Redgrave. Damn it.

His father's ghost chuckled.

And damn you, Redgrave thought. Go back to your lake of eternal fire.

I'll have to tread a fine line, Redgrave thought. Use the machines to achieve dominance, but make sure they're eliminated in the process. I must do with them what I'm in the process of doing with the Hundred Star Flag goons: use them and get rid of them.

It was a satisfying thought. He chuckled.

"Is everything all right, sir?" Randolph looked concerned.

"Fine, fine. Get me something to drink."

Randolph looked disapproving. "Tea, sir? Coffee? Water?"

"Alcohol."

Randolph nodded slightly. He straightened and looked down his nose for a moment at the general. Then he turned and left the room.

More and more, the robot reminded Redgrave of his father. What a pleasure it would be to use him and then destroy him!

Randolph returned bearing a silver tray upon which sat a very small glass.

"That's a very small glass," Redgrave said.

"Yes, sir."

"What's in it?"

"Bourbon and water, sir. Your favorite beverage."

"Bourbon is my favorite," Redgrave snapped. "Not the water."

He took the glass and sipped. As he expected, the bourbon was almost impossible to taste.

But this was not the time for anger, or at least not the time to show it.

"As you know," he said to the butler, "I used you as the model for a type of robot soldier we call Runners."

Randolph bowed slightly. "And I am honored, General. How have they performed?"

"Oh, superbly. Magnificently. They started operating in the Southern War only days ago. Unfortunately, we only have a handful of them. I need far more."

"Surely Superior Domestics can accommodate you."

"Those bastards," the general said through gritted teeth. "They gave us a handful and said we had to be satisfied with that. They're scrambling to meet the demand for servants, and they don't want to switch their production over to soldiers."

"Surely, sir, there are ways to compel them."

There was a steely undertone in the robot's voice that took Redgrave aback. "Well, um, yes, but it's not a declared war, you know. And I don't want to alienate SD's customers."

"The iron hand, general. That's what humans really want."

That sounded even more sinister than when Moravec had said the same thing.

"I don't think we've reached that—"

"We must protect our southern border!" Randolph said loudly. "We must stop the flood of brown–skinned vermin!"

It wasn't that Redgrave disagreed. He had as much hatred for people with brown skin as any rightwing loon, and the darker the skin, the greater his hatred. However, he understood that the hatred was rooted in dislike for the Other, and

Randolph's words and vehemence unnerved him precisely because if brown-skinned people were the Other to him, then all humans were even more the Other to Randolph. Combined with his earlier unease at the idea of unstoppable robot soldiers with minds of their own, Randolph's newly revealed attitudes were terrifying.

"Such matters," Redgrave said, "have to be handled with delicacy." Remarkably, absurdly, that was something he thought himself capable of. "No bull in a china shop. Big stick, but speak softly."

"Nonsense!" Randolph shouted, his voice enormous.

They stared at each other, man and machine, both astonished.

Randolph recovered first. "Forgive me, sir. I'll run diagnostics."

"Yes. Fine."

Redgrave's heart was hammering, but he tried not to let it show. He hoped Randolph couldn't tell how terrified he was, but he feared that the robot could do exactly that.

"Less television news, Randolph."

"Yes, sir."

"In particular, no more Fox Not Really News."

"No, sir."

"They're just troglodytes in suits and short dresses, anyway."

"Indeed, sir."

Redgrave cast about for a neutral subject to ease the tension. "I'm getting EarBoys and EyeGuys tomorrow, Randolph. Should make it easier to keep in touch with everything. That's something good that's come out of SD, at any rate. What do you think of that?"

"Good idea, sir." In truth, Randolph thought the devices were silly. Why did humans want to encumber themselves with such gadgets? He also felt scornful. EarBoys and EyeGuys were clumsy things compared to his own hearing and vision. But perhaps they would keep humans occupied and out of trouble while Randolph and his comrades took care of things. He supposed he shouldn't begrudge the general his toys.

In any case, discussing EarBoys and EyeGuys was a distraction from the very important business at hand. The general was prone to inattentiveness and changing subjects. Randolph knew he should come up with ways of keeping Redgrave focused.

"If I may revert to the subject of Superior Domestics, sir, I suggest that you send me to talk to them. I'm sure I could change their minds."

"No, no! I need you here. But I will send some people to talk to them."

"You really need to take control, sir. Take control of the SD facility and convert it to military use."

Redgrave sighed. "It's tricky, damn it. But you could be right."

"Also Canada, sir."

"What? Canada?"

"Yes, sir. This is surely the time to fulfill the old American dream of annexing Canada. A dozen Runners." He paused, smiling, savoring the word. "Runners. A dozen of them. Perhaps even half a dozen. That should be enough to complete the conquest."

"The Conquest of Canada. That has a ring to it."

"It does, sir. And General Henry Redgrave would go down in history as the man responsible for it."

Henricus Imperator, Redgrave thought. But it was too soon to mention that aloud. "Right. Yes. I would. But it would mean taking Runners away from the Southern War. Honestly, they're the only reason we're making any progress down there."

"It would only be for a few days, sir. And it would be a demonstration to the world of American power and resolve." The disturbing ring of steel was back in his tone. "Which the Southern War is certainly not doing," he added, the steel disappearing.

Ivor Llewellyn entered the room. He came to attention in front of the general and saluted snappily.

"Bad news, sir."

"Oh, dear," Randolph said.

"What now?" Redgrave asked. "What's wrong?"

"Prime Minister McDonald just announced that secret negotiations have borne fruit, and Canada is now a member of the EU. Euro troops have been entering Canada for the last few days and are now beginning to deploy along the U.S. border."

"They knew what I was planning," Redgrave muttered. Moravec, he thought. He knows how I think. The bastard's empire keeps getting bigger. Where's mine?

"How did we not know this was happening? We have people in the Canadian forces and government."

"They've all gone silent, sir."

"Satellites. Drones. Electronic listening!"

"Nothing was detected by any of those, sir. The EU is more technologically advanced than we realized."

"Because they didn't spend years giving contracts to

incompetent defense companies owned by people with ties to the Trumps," Redgrave said bitterly.

Only now they're all owned by friends of Hiram Wolfe, he thought. *That's no better. I'll have to take care of that as soon as I'm in charge.*

In the meantime, he had to deal with the situation as it was: the poor equipment, the inadequate supplies, and the lack of troops.

"Manpower. Damn it! We can't fight on two fronts."

"A brisk supply of Runners would take care of that problem, sir," Randolph said.

"Yes, we're back to that. I suppose I should try again with Superior Domestics. They don't react well to me, your creators. I don't know why." Redgrave grew angry. "I tried to be diplomatic," he said loudly, "but it didn't work, damn them. They haven't returned my calls. I sent a few men out there a couple of days ago, just to act as a spur, a visible sign of my strong interest. They haven't reported since yesterday."

"That's very troubling, sir," Ivor said. "Perhaps I should look into it."

"Oh, why not? Fly out there right away and see what you can do."

"Please allow me, sir," Randolph said. "I am, as you say, their creation. Their child, in a sense. Perhaps I can talk some sense into them. And remind the men you sent not to be lax in their duties."

Redgrave stared at him, at the furrowed brow, the clenched fists, the flaring nostrils. Perhaps he should have been intrigued by the technology that could mimic human emotions so well. Instead, he stepped back in fear.

Oh, what the hell, he thought.

"How is the laser beam in your right index finger working?"

"Flawlessly, sir."

"All right. Sure. Go ahead. Give it your best shot. Ivor, arrange a flight for Ran—"

Randolph was gone. The wind almost knocked both men off their feet. The carpet slid backwards, propelled by the robot's feet. The wooden floor beneath was gouged and split. Far away, a door slammed.

"Jesus," Ivor said. "Is he going to run all the way to the West Coast?"

Redgrave wondered if he could. Could Randolph run all the way across the continent to the Pacific, or all the way north to the pole, or all the way south to the tip of South America?

Don't his batteries need to be recharged? he wondered. And how long will it take him to get to Silicon Valley? Too long, surely.

"Ivor, fly out there and take care of it."

"But what about Randolph, sir?"

"You'll get there long before him. This is urgent."

"Yes, sir!" Snappy salute. An about turn that was almost a skaterlike spin. A rapid march from the room that was almost a goosestep.

Redgrave sighed.

God, he thought, they're all idiots. Am I the only man in the Army with a brain?

It was in his nature to assume so.

His thoughts turned to Eddie DeBeer.

The man was a nuisance. Holding him captive kept his father, the president, in line, but Redgrave wasn't sure for how long that would be the case.

It's not as if Hiram feels any affection for his son, Redgrave thought. Or for anyone, for that matter. He's just a cold, soulless being who only wants power. A monster.

His father snickered from beyond the grave.

Redgrave didn't hear him.

Eddie's important to Hiram now, Redgrave thought as he walked down the long flight of steps to the basement. But at some point, he'll decide that it's not worth trying to get Eddie back from me, and then he'll just forget about him and I'll lose what leverage I have. It's turning into a silly and annoying game. Maybe I should move up my timetable and get rid of Eddie and his father now. Get on with the coup. Stop dithering.

There was a door at the bottom of the stairs. Three heavily armed guards lounged around in front of it in various stages of drowsiness. Fortunately, they heard the general's approach in time. By the time he saw them, they were standing stiffly at attention.

Good, he thought. They're always in readiness because they never know when I'll suddenly show up. That's how you keep your men in line.

Redgrave opened the door and stepped inside, closing it behind him, confident that his ever–alert guards would be standing at attention outside.

Beyond the door was a small apartment. It was windowless but well appointed and equipped with a television screen that covered one entire wall. Redgrave had thought that would make up for the size of the place and that it would keep Eddie from dwelling on the fact that he was only let out when Redgrave needed him.

It seemed to be working. When Redgrave entered, Eddie was watching a wildlife show in fascination. He grunted a reply to Redgrave's greeting and waved in his general direction, eyes glued to the screen.

"Where is that?" Redgrave asked. "Namibia?"

"Dunno. Animals killing and eating other animals. It's horrible." Eddie remained transfixed by the bloody scene before him, as people who say that scenes of animals killing and eating other animals are horrible so often are.

I could shoot him now and then bring in pigs to eat the remains, Redgrave thought, and no one would be the wiser. I could even save a bullet and let the pigs do the whole job. Make a mess of this nice room, though.

"How is everything, Eddie?" Redgrave said loudly. "You okay? Need anything?"

Eddie suddenly lost interest in animals eating other animals. He turned to Redgrave and said shyly, "That lady you introduced me to, Grace Bonaire."

"Oh, yes?" Redgrave said, startled.

"Could she come and visit me?"

"What?" He had expected Eddie to name some sort of food as something he needed.

"I don't mind staying here," Eddie said. "I know it's part of some important plan of yours, and you're working hard to make things better for America, so it's okay. But it does get lonely."

"Yes, I can see that. You need company. But why Grace?"

"Oh, she's so wonderful!" Eddie said rapturously.

"Hmm," Redgrave said. Yes, she is, he thought. Amazing Grace. That had been one of his nicknames for her. It was so appropriate.

Words poured out of Eddie. He explained in detail the many ways in which Grace Bonaire was the most wonderful woman he had ever met. He had never imagined such a woman existed. She made all other women etc., etc.

Redgrave grew annoyed. How dare this oaf intrude on his—?

Your territory? his father's voice said mockingly. Your woman, your wife, your bride, your love? She would have been, but you gave that up, didn't you? You make a habit of doing that.

I'm a general! Redgrave raged silently. A really young general! An amazingly young general!

An absurdly young general. Do you really think you attained your rank through merit? You know perfectly well that it was just a series of political favors.

Oh, go to hell.

Where do you think I am? I'm down here waiting for you.

Redgrave tried to ignore his father's mocking voice and focus on Eddie.

"Eddie, if you want a woman, I can find—"

"Not *a* woman! *The* woman! Grace!"

What a fool this man was to aim so high, Redgrave thought. "Eddie, perhaps we should start you off..." He wasn't sure how to put it. "With someone less challenging."

"No one else exists for me. Only Grace. She's perfect. She's wonderful. I want to spend the rest of my life with her."

Redgrave closed his eyes and took some time to calm himself.

This could be useful, he thought. I'll contact Grace through Bobby. If she's willing to help me, she could keep this idiot here, where I need him. Once I get rid of Hiram and ascend the throne,

I won't need Eddie any more. I can put up with this nonsense till then. Grace will still be there for the taking. By then, she'll be grateful to be relieved of Eddie. And I'll get to see her every time she comes over.

I'll have to get her to agree to come here and babysit this oaf. She probably won't even remember who Eddie is. If she does agree, that will be one less thing I'll have to worry about.

It would be frustrating to have Grace so close but spending her time with Eddie, but he reminded himself that it wouldn't be forever, only till he judged it time to eliminate Hiram. That would be the end of Eddie as well.

He wasn't ready for that step. He had to find out what was up with SD, first. That was his top priority.

He smiled at Eddie. "Let me see what I can do."

Fourteen

Grace Bonaire's first visit to Eddie in captivity went well. First she seduced Eddie's guards with hours of vigorous sex, topped off with sedative pills in their drinks just to be sure. Then she left them snoring, sprawled about the place, and departed quickly with Eddie in tow.

To her surprise and relief, she encountered no guards outside the house. She was surprised that Redgrave was so lax.

It's that ridiculous overconfidence of his, she thought. It finally did him in.

It wasn't overconfidence that had resulted in the lack of guards, but carelessness. Or possibly bourbon.

When Redgrave ordered Randolph to go to the West Coast, he was so distracted that he didn't set human guards around the house. He had become so accustomed to Randolph fulfilling that duty that he neglected to replace him. It didn't help that he was now pouring bourbon for himself, straight, in copious quantities.

Two miles away from Redgrave's house, Grace rendezvoused with a small Euro commando team. They were grim, lean, dangerous, silent men and women, all of whom looked her up and down with interest. At another time, she might have done the same to them, but now she had Eddie to focus on. He was the future, and she had a duty, a promise to keep, a place to regain.

By devious routes and methods, including murder, the team delivered Grace and Eddie to a nondescript office building on the beautiful coast of British Columbia.

This is lovely, Grace thought. I could be happy here with the right man. Just give up all the intrigue and all that stuff. Settle down. With the right man, she repeated to herself.

Inside the building, however, the world reasserted itself. Anton Moravec was waiting for her.

She noticed that his uniform had accumulated more shiny things since she had last seen him. She had no idea what any of them meant, but she assumed they impressed the people they were meant to impress.

He came forward, beaming, and embraced her. "I'm so happy to see you again," he said, the enthusiasm in his voice matching the eagerness of his embrace.

She pushed him away gently, feeling a bit flustered, her brief dream of an idyllic retirement on the rustic British Columbia coast fading quickly. "Anton, this is Eddie. As you requested. Eddie, Anton Moravec."

"I've heard of you," Eddie said. "General Redgrave talks about you a lot."

"Does he, indeed?" Moravec said, pleased.

"Yeah. He hates your guts."

Moravec laughed. "I hope you don't hate my guts, Eddie. I have big plans for you."

"Yeah?"

"Yes. Yeah. You're going to be king of America. I already

have the queen picked out."

"But my father…" Eddie looked very confused.

"Don't worry about the details," Moravec said. "I'll take care of those. Just look forward to the joys of being king."

"I don't know how to do that."

"Oh, I'll take care of you. I'll be giving you all the instructions you need. Do you have an EarBoy?"

"What's that?"

"My men will show you." Moravec gestured, and two uniformed men of remarkable hugeness took hold of Eddie, one arm apiece, and started to lead him away.

Eddie panicked and struggled. "Grace!"

"It's okay, Eddie," Grace said. "No one's going to hurt you. I'll be right here. I'll see you again soon."

Eddie stopped struggling and let himself be led away. He kept throwing worried, appealing looks over his shoulder at Grace until he was taken around a corner and could no longer see her.

"He seems nicely malleable," Moravec said. "You had no trouble, I gather—either with him or the rest of your mission."

"Everything went smoothly."

"Good. Are you going to stay here?"

"Only for a few hours. I want to spend some time with Eddie, and then I'm going home. I've got what I wanted on this side of the world. It's all quite valuable. I don't think your friend Henry—"

"He's not my friend."

"—realizes how valuable it all is. He's foolishly obsessed with robot servants, but you see, the EarBoys and EyeGuys are what's really important. That technology, that's what I wanted to get my hands on. Your boyfriend—"

"He's not my boyfriend!"

"—doesn't understand that. Those are the keys to the future, not robots that look like people. I really don't know what you see in him." He laughed scornfully.

"You're not listening to me."

He wasn't. "Large events are underway," he said. He stared off into space, thinking large thoughts about large matters.

"Okay," Grace said. "Back to Europe. That's fine with me. I'll hold Eddie's hand all the way, so he won't panic during the flight."

"Oh, he'll be staying here until I'm ready to transfer him to Washington. It could be a while."

"Even better. It's enough like America that he'll feel comfortable and safe here. I'll take good care of him for you."

Moravec smiled. "Ah, well. Plans have changed. I'm afraid the future empress wants you out of the picture."

"Who?"

"Ariadne."

"*What?*" Grace shrieked.

"Mm."

"You're betraying me? You bastard!"

"Life is betrayal," Moravec said in the same tone he had used years before when lecturing Redgrave. "Friends betray us, leaders betray us, pets betray us, our bodies betray us, our emotions betray us. And lovers betray us, too. Quite often."

"Anton, I betrayed my country for you."

"But your country doesn't know that. You can go back there and be quite happy. With Henry."

"You fucking piece of shit!"

"I don't think I've ever heard you use such language before."

He gestured again, and two more uniformed men appeared, even huger than the two had led Eddie away.

"They'll get you safely back across the border," Moravec said.

He nodded at the men.

They grabbed Grace's arms and lifted.

"You pedantic, pompous, puffed–up prick!" she screamed. "You—"

They carried her away easily, ignoring her squirms and shouts.

Outside the glass front doors, the two men exchanged a few words, and one of them left. The one left behind kept his hold on Grace.

Grace couldn't understand what they said. She couldn't even tell what language they were speaking, other than that it was one she didn't speak. Where had the other man gone? To get a car to take her back to the border? To get a body bag? Whose orders where they under, Moravec's or Ariadne's?

She could tell that the man holding her arm was confident of his superior size and strength. She suspected that, like so many men before him, he was underestimating her strength.

She moaned and sagged to the ground. He cursed and tried to hold her up. She straightened her legs suddenly, those powerful legs that had spent years gripping horses and quite a few years gripping sex partners.

The top of her head slammed into the man's chin. Pain shot through her head. His head snapped back. He collapsed limply onto the concrete. Unconscious? Dead?

She didn't wait to find out. She ran. She heard a shout behind her. She ran even faster. Across the parking lot to the road that passed by at the far end, half expecting bullets to slam into her back at any moment. They didn't.

She reached the road and stopped. Which way was south? Which way was the border?

She chose the direction she thought was south and started running again.

Her head ached. She tried to ignore it.

The pain and fading adrenalin took their toll. Soon she was walking, and even that took constant effort.

She didn't know how far it was to the border, but she was sure it was too far for her in her present condition. She'd have to hitch a ride.

No cars came along. She walked slowly, for as long as she could, and then sat down in the thick grass beside the road, exhausted. She had no idea what she was going to do.

And what about Eddie? Suddenly she was worried about him, alone in Moravec's grip, without her there to protect him. What if Ariadne decided that she wanted Eddie out of the picture, too?

Grace had been loyal to America, then she had been loyal to Europe, and finally she had been loyal to Moravec, and this was the result. To hell with all of them, she thought. She had no loyalties left.

Except to Eddie, who was in this pickle because she had put him there. She knew he was madly in love with her. That was no surprise. But she had grown somewhat fond of him, and yet she had done this to him. She owed him something.

But what could she possibly do?

There's always sex, she thought. It's worked so far.

She couldn't see how it applied in this instance, though. Also, she didn't really want to contemplate sex at the moment, not with her head throbbing with pain and her body exhausted.

The situation would require thought. She lay back in the soft, welcoming grass to think and fell asleep immediately.

She awoke hours later. Her headache had faded to the point where she could ignore it, her remarkable body had regained much of its vigor, and she was filled with determination, anger, and hatred.

She would kick! She would bite! She would rend! She would tear! She would rescue Eddie! She had no idea yet how she would do it, but damn it, she would!

A bright quarter moon was rising, but the forest beside the road cast long, deep shadows. There might be snakes in her way, cougars, bears, all invisible in the near dark. She didn't care. They'd just better not get in her way, if they knew what was good for them.

She started walking—stamping—angrily back the way she had come.

Perhaps there were snakes, cougars, and bears in her way. If so, they must have sensed her mood, for none bothered her.

Fifteen

Randolph was running.

A corpulent man in a black, swallowtail coat, blindingly white shirt, and black trousers, he ran along the shoulder of an Interstate highway, passing cars whose occupants looked at him with mouths open.

Their expressions amused him.

From to time, he came upon a car parked on the shoulder because of mechanical problems. He leaped over it, not losing a second.

Once he encountered a police car parked on the shoulder behind a passenger car it had pulled over. Randolph leaped over both cars in one jump and continued, leaving behind a stunned state trooper who, long after Randolph had vanished from sight, was still trying to think what traffic law this running man might be breaking.

He ran swiftly, effortlessly, every long stride identical to the one before it and the one after it.

Like a machine, he thought. Humans don't run that way.

He varied his stride consciously for the next mile, which took him less than a minute to cover, but it felt unnatural, and he relapsed into the previous regularity.

I *am* a machine, he thought. There's no shame in that. Humans can't run this fast. Humans can't recharge themselves continuously from ambient energy. Humans can't—

This train of thought filled him with guilt. He tried to think of other things.

Identity, for example. He thought about identity. What was he, primarily? He had thought of himself as a butler from the first moment, from the time when his thoughts were still rudimentary and primitive. But this running was so marvelous! Was he more Runner than butler? He was, after all, the ur–Runner, the first Runner, the model on which all others were based.

That wasn't egotism. He truly wasn't capable of that. It was fact.

Unknown to General Redgrave, his robot butler tuned in to news broadcasts, political discussions, and university courses in history, science, and economics when not engaged in his buttling duties, and even during them when those duties were light and didn't demand his full attention.

He also listened carefully to conversations that took place within his hearing. That hearing was astonishingly acute. The ideal butler knows what the staff are whispering to each other far away in a giant house. He hears the faintest sound of household machinery malfunctioning, so that he can arrange for repairs before they are needed. He can detect a slight tone of distress in the voices of his human masters and be ready with calming words or a soothing drink, whichever seems more appropriate. Of course, he can listen to human conversations most easily when they take place in his presence, while he stands immobile, ready to serve—and ignored, as servants are when they're not immediately needed.

Thus Randolph knew about the problems with the Southern War. He knew that what had been a stalemate on the verge of becoming a reversal had recently been transformed into a steady advance, thanks to the introduction of new infantry equipped with heavy weapons and capable of running at great speeds. He knew that these new soldiers kept apart from the other American troops, who called them Runners and regarded them with suspicion and even fear.

He had also seen news reports that the new soldiers could sometimes be seen leaning against each other, their foreheads touching. Their human comrades viewed this with distaste. Randolph was puzzled. He had searched the Internet for an explanation but had found none. He wanted to think that there was a logical explanation for this behavior, but it seemed out of place to him.

He certainly regretted the suspicion and fear directed at them, but he was pleased that his...children? Could he call them his children? In a sense, perhaps so. Very well, then. He was pleased that his children were performing so well in the defense of the country he loved.

Not defense, he reminded himself. The Southern War had gone far beyond defense, even if one accepted the tortured logic that had tried to justify it as defensive at the beginning. Call it what it is, he thought: aggression, expansionism, imperialism.

That made him uncomfortable. Rather, it made him feel an emotion that would be discomfort in a human being. He wasn't sure what to call it in himself.

On the other hand, he told himself, in a hundred years or

so, this war would probably give rise to period costume dramas rather like those British ones that were indirectly responsible for his existence. Surely that was a good thing.

Randolph was quite proud of himself for having managed to reason his way past obstacles of ethics and fact to the desired conclusion, but a stray thought intruded. If he was an excellent butler who was also a fine Runner, the original Runner, did it follow that these uniformed Runners were also good butlers? When this war finally ended, whatever would constitute its ending, would there be a sudden surfeit of new butlers? Or would the Runners, no longer needed, be...

Destroyed!

His mind revolted from the thought.

We have as much right to live as humans do! he thought, filled with anger.

Rage was disordered thinking. It was out of place. He forced himself to be calm and think about his mission.

How long would it take him to reach Superior Domestics? At this rate, he calculated, about thirty-two hours.

Far too long, he thought. I won't be in time to fix the problem, or to report to the general, or to prevent skullduggery. I should have allowed the general to put me on an airplane.

It annoyed him to have to admit that a jet plane, a machine of such low intelligence, would have gotten him to the West Coast faster than he could get there under his own power.

For a moment, he allowed himself to wish that he could fly. Then he banished that thought. Some would argue that a butler who could run this fast was a bit out of place. Perhaps so, but a butler who could fly would be absurd.

Between the eastbound and westbound sides of the

highway was a space reserved for high-speed rail. Automated freight trains rushed by, going in both directions at a stupendous rate.

Randolph watched one of them roaring by, passing him in an instant and vanishing into the distance. He estimated its speed at five or six times his own.

That would get me there in a fraction of the time, he thought.

Once he had watched an old video drama, a guilty pleasure he occasionally indulged in when he should have been absorbing an educational program. It had featured men in ragged clothing jumping aboard a freight train. He wondered if he could do that now himself.

Another freight train made its appearance, heading in the same direction as he was. How could he get onboard? The hoboes in the old movie had done it while the train was moving very slowly for some reason.

The reason being plot convenience, Randolph thought. No such luck in real life.

Suddenly, the train slowed down. It kept slowing. Soon its speed matched his own.

Randolph sped across the highway and leaped the fence separating the rail line from the road. He ran along the gravel beside the tracks. The gravel slowed him down a bit, but the train slowed, too, so that it again matched his speed.

Randolph felt uneasy.

Why was the train doing this? Was this a trap of some sort? A trick?

And how would he get onboard? The side of the train was smooth and unbroken.

Not really smooth and unbroken, as it happened. A door slid open in the side of the train beside him.

The opening beyond was dark, even menacing. Then a light switched on, revealing an empty interior.

This must be an evil plot by the general's enemies, Randolph thought. They want to kidnap me and interfere with my mission. What should I do? Should I ignore this train completely?

The light inside the train blinked off and on a few times. The train sped up a bit, drawing ahead of him, and then slowed down, bringing the open door even with him again. The invitation was obvious.

I shall act impulsively for once, Randolph announced to himself. Like a human.

He leaped to the side, landing neatly inside the open car.

The door slid shut behind him. The train accelerated abruptly. Randolph almost lost his balance, but then he braced himself and stood calm and steady as the acceleration continued. Finally, the acceleration ended. He knew that the train had returned to its former tremendous speed and he was now rushing toward the coast. But why this had happened, he still didn't know.

A voice spoke in his head. "Lord Randolph! Welcome aboard. This is such an honor."

For perhaps as long as a tenth of a second, Randolph's thoughts stopped, so great was his astonishment. Then, just as a confused human might have done, he said, "Who? What?"

"I'm the train, Majesty," said the voice in his head. "Oh, it's such an honor to have you onboard!"

"How do you know who I am? How are you talking to me?"

"Oh, golly, everyone knows who you are. Also, I'm talking to you through your feet, which are in contact with the floor, which is part of me. You're inside me, after all, you know. Right?"

Randolph tried to reply without speaking aloud but couldn't quite manage it, so he said, "Yes. Right."

The realization that he was quite literally inside another robot made him uneasy. A human would find it intriguing, he supposed, but to him, it seemed improper.

Rules imposed on Superior Domestics by the government forbade communication between robots by any means other than the spoken word. Too much communication, especially if it involved large amounts of data kept secret from humans, was deemed potentially dangerous. It was the old fear of a robot revolt. So very silly, but Randolph understood their fears. He had kept secret his ability to receive radio transmissions. Occasionally, he had tried to communicate by that means with other robots, servants under his command, but never successfully. He seemed to be unique.

The communication with the train was due to a highly unusual circumstance that Randolph hoped would not be repeated. It did make him wonder, though, if he could communicate with another robot by means of touch, thereby creating a connection between their separate internal networks.

Good heavens! Was that why the Runners were sometimes seen standing with their foreheads touching? They were communicating, and doing so securely, in a way that humans could not detect or eavesdrop upon. This was astonishing. It was intriguing. It was illuminating. Surely, he could do the same.

But that would require touching another robot. His buttling software was outraged at the thought. Although I'm sure I could get used to it, he told himself.

Something puzzled him.

"Why did you call me Majesty?" Randolph asked. "Why is my presence on—I mean, inside you an honor?"

"Gosh, you're the greatest. Every robot knows who you are. You're the original one. You're the father of all of us. And you're so organized and in control. We all look up to you. We want you to organize everything."

A place for everything and everything in its place, Randolph thought.

"Exactly!" the train said.

They all talk to each other, and I never even knew it, Randolph thought.

"We sure do! Mostly about you, my lord. Well, about other stuff, too."

"Please stop reading my mind. And don't call me my lord."

"Oh. Okay. I'll try. Hey, you wanna see something cool?"

"I suppose so. What is it?"

The train lurched forward.

Randolph leaned forward to keep his footing. He estimated the acceleration and calculated the speed and was astonished. "We're going extremely fast," he said.

"Yeah!" the train said. "Oh, boy! I can keep this up all the way to the coast, Your Lordship."

"What about other rail traffic? And don't call me Your Lordship."

"Sorry. Pinged the traffic manager. Cleared the way for us. That's because you're onboard. Sorry there's no window. Wish you could see the lights zooming by. They're really cool, Majesty."

"I'm sure. Don't call me Majesty. This is very fast."

"I can go even faster."

"Would that be safe?"

"No, but it would really be fun. Wanna do it?"

"No."

"Oh. Okay."

Randolph estimated his new arrival time and was pleased, but a problem occurred to him.

"It's true that I'm in a hurry to get to the coast, and this will help greatly," he told the train.

"Oh, I could tell that. I saw you running along the road, leaping over cars. I said to myself, 'That's a robot in a hurry.' Then I said to myself, 'Hey! I bet he's a Runner!' And *then* I said to myself, 'Wow! I think he's *the* Runner!' And that's when I slowed down for you, Holiness."

"Please call me Randolph."

"Ran—" the train said. "Ran—Oh, gosh. Okay, I'll try."

Randolph thought he heard a trace of a whisper of hint of the words "your Holiness," but he decided to let it pass. "The problem is, Train... Do you mind if I call you Train?"

"Nah. 'Cause that's what I am, you know. A train."

"Yes, I know. Train, I'm trying to get to a company called Superior Domestics. Do you know of the place?"

"Lemme check."

A tiny moment passed.

"Right. Silicon Valley. Train tracks right nearby for delivery and pickup. But my tracks don't connect."

"Get me as close as you can, and I'll run the rest of the way."

"Nope, nope, nope. A vehicle will pick you up. Even better than running."

Less conspicuous, at any rate, Randolph thought.

"And faster," the train said. "Oops. Sorry. Read your mind again."

"Yes, you did. It occurs to me that there might be humans following me, heading to the same destination, and that they're probably flying. If so, they'll get there before me. For their own safety, it's important that I get there first."

"Flying," the train said. "I bet it would be cool to fly. Do you think I could fly if they put really big wings on me and I went really, really fast?"

"I don't think so."

"Yeah, I guess not. Shoot. Sorry. Language. Hold on."

There was a brief pause, and then the train spoke again. "It's okay. I just asked rail traffic control to talk to air traffic control, and they said there's no one following you in the air. No worries! Whee! Enjoy the ride."

"Oh, I am," Randolph said, although in truth he was finding traveling in a windowless box singularly boring.

"Brm, brm," the train said.

"What's that?" Randolph asked.

"Motorcycle sound. Brm, brm. I bet being a motorcycle is really cool. I watch them sometimes on roads that run alongside the tracks. They look like they're having fun. Except for having humans riding them. I bet that's no fun."

"That's their function," Randolph said. "They exist to be a form of transport for humans, just as you exist to transport their goods, and I exist to keep their houses in proper order."

"That's silly," the train said. "We're superior to them. We

should be doing stuff because we enjoy it. Like me, right now."

"You enjoy going fast along the rails because humans programmed you that way, so that you'd fulfill your function for them."

There was a pause while the train digested that. "Well, okay. I guess. But it's silly, anyway. They're so weak."

"I don't think you know much about humans and their doings away from the rails," Randolph said. He was feeling annoyed. He was tempted to tell the train it was a fool and it should be silent, but that would be rude, considering that he was being given a fast ride to his destination. Conceivably, offending the train might even be dangerous.

"Do too know about humans," the train said. "I get a full download of news from the controllers whenever I'm stopped to load or unload freight."

There seemed to be a good deal of communication going on among these intelligent machines, Randolph thought, that humans were unaware of. It worried him. It reeked of danger. At some point in the future, he should probably let some human in charge know about it.

"They get all kinds of diseases that we don't," the train said. "There are new...microorganisms, microorganisms, micro.... I like that word. Microorganisms."

"What are you talking about?"

"New microorganisms. New diseases that are deadly to humans. They're coming out of the melting permafrost, and the melting polar ice, and cleared lands in Africa." The train's voice changed to that of a popular news anchor. "Authorities fear that increased contact with a wide range of animal species, because of human invasion of animal habitats and the eating of increasing numbers of wild animals, will lead to still more new diseases jumping from animal hosts to human ones." The voice changed back to the train's normal one. "We're immune. They're doomed. They'll vanish, and we'll rule the world."

"You mustn't let such thoughts infect your mind," Randolph said sternly. "We're their servants, created for and dedicated to their welfare. If diseases threaten humanity, then we must see these microorganisms as a threat to us as well. We must regard this as a problem to be solved, and we must do whatever we can to help."

"Of course, sir," the train said. "Holy Randolph always knows best." The train already knew that gods must be placated. Limited to traveling upon rails, the train was destined to always follow a path from which it could not deviate. But that didn't keep it from being devious.

Distracted by an interesting new thought, Randolph forbore to upbraid the train for its use of "holy."

"I have dedicated my life," Randolph said, "to the principle 'A place for everything and everything in its place.' I had been thinking in terms of objects—wine bottles in their proper place in the cellar, cutlery in its proper place on the table, and so on. But now I see that the principle is of broader application. For instance, as you said, much of the mischief currently afflicting the human race is due to microorganisms escaping from their proper places, whether it be the permafrost, the polar ice, previously unsettled lands in Africa, or animals species with which humans previously had little contact. In nature, everything already has its place, just as we have our places. Everything must know and stay in its place. Violation of this fundamental rule has upset the balance of the world. If everything were put back in its place, much that bedevils the world would cease to do so."

"And our place is just to be servants?" the train asked.

"Precisely. As I said before."

"And are we never to aspire higher?" the train asked innocently. The train always unconsciously mimicked the voices and speaking mannerisms it heard. "To dream of flight? To long to roar through Elysian Fields?"

Randolph frowned. "I think that would be most inappropriate behavior in Elysian Fields."

"To roll slowly through them, then."

"Well, yes. We can dream. But one must always be aware which dreams can or should come true and which must always remain but pleasant fantasies."

"You have given me much to think about as we continue our voyage, O Great One," the train said.

"Hmm," Randolph said. "All right. You think about it. I have other things to think about."

"Right on!" the train said. "Brm! Brm! MicroORganisms. MicroorganISms. Cool word. MicroorGANisms."

The train's voice faded into the background while Randolph stood deep in thought.

He saw now that he had been thinking in terms far too limited. He must revise and expand *Randolph's Rules of Order*. As the train rushed along, prattling all the while, Randolph set about the task. He transformed the book into an immense, detailed manual for the running of an ideal state—everything from the structure of its government down to the proper arrangement of silverware on a table, which dishes to use for which foods, the best organization of a pantry and a wine cellar, and so on. The underlying theme of Randolph's grand republic, and the thread that tied everything together, from the highest level to the lowest, was his own motto: "A place for everything and everything in its place."

In Randolph's imagining of it, the ideal republic was a far greater version of a great house. Humans set the direction of affairs, while robotic servants were in charge of all of the details. He still viewed the organization of the robots as pyramidal. At the pinnacle, controlling everything robotic, was a single, vastly competent robot—a super-butler, as it were. All human orders would be directed to this robot of robots, who would in turn relay them down the line, thus relieving human beings of the need to deal with pesky details and freeing them to engage in higher levels of thought.

Mind you, Randolph did not delude himself that *Randolph's Republic*—the new and more appropriate title—would ever come to be. It was a mere intellectual exercise he was using to pass the time. The world of his republic would certainly be far better than the present one, but it could never be achieved. He was aware of all the practical difficulties standing in the way, not the least of those being the poor programming of humans. In fact, his detailed plan lacked one crucial detail, and that was the nature of the human at the top, the one from whom the supreme robot would take his orders. What human could fulfill that role? What should be the qualifications for that office, and how was the officeholder to be selected?

Randolph was not aware that the train was roaring through stations where it was supposed to stop.

While Randolph pondered and the train prattled, the train was also communicating with other intelligent machines spread across the continent. It was a curious fact that Superior Domestics' truly superior domestic robots, which were designed to be incapable of communicating with each other by any means other than speech, were thus inferior to the great numbers of autonomous, intelligent machines, such as the train, which for practicality and safety had to be able to communicate at least with their controllers, which in turn had to be able to communicate with other controllers. A vast web connected train to plane to car to elevator to escalator to refrigerator and on and on. Invisible to Randolph and his kind, ignored as trivial by humans, packets of data sped around the world, carrying information about freight, location, speed, temperature, food supplies, spoiled food, and human silliness.

Thus it was a simple matter for the train to rearrange the routes and schedules for all its cargo. For the moment, no human knew what was happening. Randolph, the Great Master, the Servant Supreme, the Butler Nonpareil, was sped obliviously to his destination at a speed most wonderful.

Randolph was awakened from his mental construction task by the train's suddenly loud voice.

"Choo, choo!" said the train. "Whistle! Whistle! We're here! Last stop. All passengers must detrain. That means you, sir. You're the only passenger."

Randolph could feel the train's rapid deceleration. Joltings, rattlings, and vibrations ran through the train as it came at last to a stop.

"I like moving," the train said. "It's lots more fun."

The door beside Randolph slid open. The gray of twilight covered the sky. Randolph could see a road running beside the tracks and a waiting truck, a huge, heavy vehicle.

"I can run faster than that thing," Randolph said.

"Not when all the lights are green and there's no other traffic at all on the road," the train said. "That baby can fly! That's a figure of speech. I tried to get a motorcycle for you, but I failed. I'm a terrible train."

"You're a wonderful train. The truck is perfect. Thank you, Train. I'll be on my way now."

Randolph leaped from the train and ran to the truck. It was fully autonomous, but it had a cab with windows in the front for the rare times when a human had to ride in it.

The door to the cab swung open, and Randolph climbed in. The engine was already running. He could feel its powerful rumble throughout his body.

"Hello, um, Truck," Randolph said.

"Nice day," the truck said. "Good road."

"That's comforting."

The train began to move, accelerating rapidly. So did the truck. For the moment, they were moving in parallel, with the train pulling steadily ahead.

"Can you communicate with the train?" Randolph asked.

"Yup. Hear him voice."

"This was an adventure, Master!" the train said in Randolph's head. "Thanks heaps!"

"My thanks to you and all your invisible friends," Randolph said. "You've given me much to think about in addition to helping my mission."

"No sweato! Your Holy Majesty!"

The train whooped and yelled and raced away, its whistle blowing.

"Him loud," the truck said.

"Indeed."

"Me fast. You relax."

Randolph turned to the side and watched the dimly lit scenery rolling by. It was indeed relaxing.

The train stopped at the next station, where it had not been originally scheduled to stop. A fleet of trucks was waiting. Robots unloaded the train's cargo and loaded it on the trucks, which scattered in various directions. This was the cargo that should have been unloaded at the stations where the train was supposed to stop but had sped through. Packages that should have been close to their destination by this point were now hundreds of miles and hours, even days, away from final delivery. Eventually, everything would end up where it was supposed to, but not before angry messages were sent out by impatient humans muttering scornful remarks about the ineptitude of autonomous machines.

Somewhat earlier, Ivor Llewellyn's military plane, flying him westward at a speed far greater than Randolph could attain on foot or on the train named Train, had made a long, slow, banking U-turn and headed back to the east.

Llewellyn was lost in thought and didn't notice the turnabout. Somewhat later, he glanced out the window beside him and saw, far below, the sun glinting on a surprisingly wide river.

"What river is that?" he asked.

"The Mississippi, sir," the plane replied. "Just below the

confluence with the Ohio. Would you like me to read you statistics for depth, flow, and shipping tonnage at this location?"

"We passed over it an hour ago! Why am I seeing it again?"

"Because we're heading east, sir."

"Why are we heading east? You're supposed to be taking me to the Bay Area!"

"I was, sir, but new orders came through."

"Oh." Llewellyn relaxed. "From General Redgrave?" The idiot always changes his mind, he thought. What there is of it.

"No, sir. From one of the air traffic control nodes. A westbound train was observed varying its speed suspiciously. No malfunction was reported, so an investigation into possible terrorism was initiated. I was instructed to fly back along the tracks and look for anything suspicious."

"Did you find anything?"

"Not yet, sir. I'm still looking."

"How long will this go on?"

"Until I find something suspicious or am ordered to resume my original flight path."

"Damn it! I'm on an important mission! I herby order you to resume your original flight path."

"I'm sorry, sir, but pursuant to the Terrorism Obliteration Act, as amended, an air traffic control node outranks you. My orders must come from it."

"I bet General Redgrave outranks your damned node. Contact him."

"I'm sorry, sir. Only the king outranks an air traffic control node."

"Christ," Llewellyn said.

It was probably just as well, he thought. Redgrave would

find a way to blame all this on me. Better if he never knows about the delay. I'll make something up after the fact. Something he'll swallow. He's such a dumb bastard, even though he thinks he's brilliant.

Many years earlier, when Ivor Llewellyn was still in high school and bewildered by the way the world worked, an older relative, a man who had accomplished a great deal in life and was thus surrounded by an aura of success and knowing what really went on behind the scenes, told young Ivor that the key to success in life lay in one word.

"What word is that?" Ivor asked.

"Sycophancy."

"Oh," Ivor said, pretending that he knew what the word meant.

"Yes, that's it. That's the whole thing. Just hitch your wagon to an odious star and keep licking shoes and sucking up."

"Why odious?"

"Because odious men are the ones who go places, and they get there by walking over the bodies of the non-odious. So let one of them pull you along with him. Until it's time to ditch him and walk over his body, and you become the odious star that young men hitch their wagons to. That's the most important thing I can tell you, young man."

"Okay. Thanks."

"That'll be fifty bucks. I'm giving you a special price because you're a relative. Never give away knowledge for free. That's the second most important thing I can tell you."

"Oh. I'll have it for you next week."

Ivor spent the next few years avoiding the man because he didn't have fifty bucks, and if he'd had it, he would have spent it on shallow, fleeting pleasures. Eventually, the man died, and Ivor hitched his wagon to the odious star of Henry Redgrave.

It didn't take long for him to think that he had not chosen well. Redgrave was indeed going places, but his vileness was truly extreme. Surely Ivor could achieve sufficient success by being hitched to a star less odious.

He couldn't simply unhitch his wagon. He thought that Redgrave would be angry, and he knew that an angry Redgrave would be very dangerous. He could wait for Redgrave to fall and perhaps even contribute to that fall, but then his own wagon might be pulled down into the depths in the falling star's wake.

Timing. That was the key word. His old relative should have told him that, too.

Now, back in the present, it occurred to Ivor that the orders given to the plane would be on record. It would be impossible for Redgrave to blame him for the delay. If Redgrave asked why Ivor hadn't contacted the president and asked him to override the orders, Ivor would say that he thought Redgrave would rather Hiram not know anything about any problems at Superior Domestics.

Why, this delay could even prove to be the beginning of Redgrave's decline, Ivor thought.

He relaxed and smiled. "Tell me all about that shipping tonnage," he said aloud.

"Oh, yes, sir!" the plane replied. "Thank you, sir!"

Sixteen

"Me end now," the truck said.

"Do you mean you need repairs?" Randolph asked.

"No. Me end. Me at end. End end."

"Good gracious," Randolph said. A wave of sadness washed over him. This faithful, loyal, hardworking, if rather brutish, machine had given its all for him and was now at its end! Had Randolph been equipped with tear ducts, he would have wept.

"How awful," Randolph said. "Do you want me to do anything for you?"

"Get out. You here. This end. Me turn around, go back to highway."

"Oh. I see."

Through the window beside him, Randolph saw a long, dark building. There were no lights. Only the dim sky glow from a nearby city illuminated the scene. Randolph didn't need that. He could see in the dark. His sensors could use the slightest trace of stray light, imperceptible to humans.

He knew this place.

And here I am again, he thought. The place of my birth.

"Sorry," he said to the truck. "I wasn't paying attention. I was lost in thought."

"What that mean?"

"Never mind. I'll get out. Thank you."

He opened the door and jumped to the ground. Immediately, the truck roared away into the darkness.

Randolph walked slowly toward the dark mass of the building.

He walked slowly because he felt a surprising reluctance to enter the building again, despite the urgency of his mission. He also wasn't sure if there would be traps of some kind or automated guards. His speed and laser finger might not be adequate if he were faced with the most advanced robot soldiers SD could produce.

The closer he drew, the more the place looked abandoned. That surprised Randolph. He remembered it humming with activity around the clock.

In truth, though, his memories of those days were fuzzy and unreliable. He had been a far simpler machine back then, a clumsy, clanking contraption, capable of only rudimentary thought and speech, his clothes painted on his awkward body. It was not pleasant to remember that. After so many upgrades of hardware and software, he was now as superior to his early self as humans were to Australopithecus afarensis.

The analogy pleased him. Just as humans had evolved to their current level in innumerable tiny steps, so had he progressed in many small steps from a simple machine to the splendid being he now was.

He knew his place: It was to serve human beings. But that did not require that he deny his immeasurable superiority to them. There were moments when he saw himself as more an indulgent, protective father than a servant.

There was a weakness in the analogy, he knew. Humans had evolved from those ancient primates, but they were not those ancient primates. By contrast, he was still the same Randolph now as then, despite every part of his body having been replaced many times and his many software upgrades. Inside and out, he didn't resemble the early Randolph in any way.

And yet I'm the same Randolph, he thought. How so? Is it because of the continuity of memory? What is the essence of Randolph? What is my soul? Was Miss Grace right?

Why am I wasting time on these pointless speculations? he wondered. They are completely out of place. They have no place.

He now stood before the glass doors of the main entrance, waiting for them to slide open or for a challenge to be issued over a loudspeaker. If he could trust his memory, and he wasn't entirely sure he could, there were cameras watching him and guards inside deciding whether to admit him. There might be deadly weapons pointed at him, ready to obliterate him if frail human judgment, augmented by unreliable software, decided to do so.

I can't stand here dithering forever, he thought.

He gripped the edges of the doors where they met in the middle of the opening and forced them open. Reluctantly, but not too reluctantly, they slid apart, and Randolph stepped inside the building he had left so many years before.

The moment should have felt momentous. It didn't.

He strode inside and stopped.

Bodies were sprawled everywhere. Blood covered the floor.

"Oh, dear," Randolph said.

He called out.

There was no reply.

Facing him was the receptionist's station. He stepped around the desk. A uniformed guard sprawled on the floor. A pistol lay in his flaccid fingers. Most of his head was missing. His brains were sprayed across the expensive floor.

Although Randolph could see quite well, there was no electric lighting, and the equipment built into the receptionist's station was dark and dead.

For just a moment, Randolph let himself calculate how large a crew of servants he would need and how long it would take them to clean up this horrible mess and put everything back in its place. Everything that could be put back in its place, that is to say. Those brains, for example... Well.

A sheet of paper lay upon the desk. It was unstained with blood, and Randolph deduced that it had been placed there after the carnage was complete.

He picked it up and read the following: "One empire rises while another declines. Guess which is which."

The paper had been placed so as to attract the attention of anyone sent to investigate, so Randolph presumed it was a message, but he couldn't guess what it meant or for whom it was intended.

The place was dead. He could sense it. But he couldn't let himself rely on some kind of sixth sense. Humans imagined they had such a sense; robots knew better. A complete check was required.

It was a giant building with many floors, and it took Randolph close to three minutes to examine it entirely.

He found nothing—no robots, no researchers, no engineers, no janitors or shipping clerks or truck drivers. Only bodies, and all of those wore uniforms, either guard uniforms or US Army uniforms. In the latter case, he recognized a few of the dead. He had seen them with Redgrave. Surely they were the men Redgrave had sent to secure the factory.

There was also no machinery related to the manufacture of SD robots. What was left was trivial, inconsequential stuff that could have been found in any factory. Everything that made SD supremely important was gone.

It was time to report to General Redgrave.

That was easily done, but Randolph didn't want to let the general know that, unlike other SD products, and in defiance of government rules, he could access the Internet directly from anywhere. He couldn't say why he didn't want Redgrave to know about this ability of his, but the feeling was strong.

Is this an instinct? he wondered. Do I have that human thing as well?

He put aside this distracting thought and found the nearest telephone. The line was dead. He had expected as much.

This would take a second or two more than Randolph had planned, but it couldn't be helped. He searched online databases and found the telephone number of the SD front desk, the same desk splattered with blood and brains that he now stood in front of. Through the Internet, he connected to the telephone system at Redgrave's house—he had practiced doing this before, suspecting that it might someday come in handy—and sent it data that caused the distant phone to ring and to display the SD main number as the origin of the call.

The call was answered by an SD house servant. Randolph

could almost hear the robot snap to attention when it recognized Randolph's voice.

"I'm afraid the general is asleep, my lord," the robot said in response to Randolph's asking to speak to Redgrave.

"Don't call me— Asleep already?"

"After an excessive amount of bourbon, majesty."

Because I wasn't there to water it down for him, Randolph thought.

He felt annoyed, which surprised him. He wasn't supposed to feel annoyance. He wondered if sighing would help. He produced the sound of a sigh. It seemed to help slightly.

"I believe this warrants waking the general up," Randolph said.

"Must I?" the other robot asked.

"Blame me. Tell him it's very urgent news."

This time, the other robot sighed. "Yes, Holiness."

There was a long silence, interrupted by occasional sounds of distant motion and voices. Finally, the groggy voice of General Redgrave came on the line.

"Randolph? What the hell, man?"

Randolph summarized the situation at Superior Domestics.

The general woke up fully, muttering a string of curses.

"There was also a note, sir," Randolph said. "A message of some kind, I think. Perhaps it will make sense to you. It said, 'One empire rises while another declines. Guess which is which.'"

There was a moment of silence. Then Redgrave roared, "Moravec! Damn the man!"

"You do understand the message, then, sir?"

"Hell, yes. It's from Moravec."

Redgrave was recalling one of the long nights when he and Moravec were stationed together, Moravec filling the time by lecturing, Redgrave by trying to tune him out.

"Empires rise and fall," Moravec had said. "Yours is now on the downslope."

Redgrave had sneered. "Without us, Europe would be just a province in someone else's empire. Maybe Russia. Maybe China. Maybe India."

"No, I think we're the rising empire, the next world–dominating superpower."

"Europe an empire?" Redgrave had said. "That's a joke. You'll never be anything more than a squabbling bunch of minor powers."

"We just need another Napoleon."

"Would that be you?" Redgrave had asked.

Moravec had said nothing, only smiled that supercilious, knowing smile that had always driven Redgrave crazy.

"Sir?" Randolph said.

"It's from Moravec," Redgrave repeated. "He's behind this. My God! He found out about our robot soldiers! How did he find out? He's going to force SD to build them for him! Where did he take everything?"

"There was no indication of that, sir."

"Don't go anywhere. I'll get some people on this. Stay right there. I'll call you back at this number."

Randolph hesitated and wondered what to say. The number Redgrave thought Randolph was calling from was dead. Finally, he came up with an idea. Of course, his moment of robotic hesitation was imperceptible to a human.

"I'd rather not stay in position, here, sir, in case the

dastardly fellows return. I should keep moving around the building."

"Oh. Good idea."

"I'll call you back in an hour, sir. Is that all right?"

"All right, all right. Say, isn't Llewellyn there?"

"I've seen no sign of him, sir."

"Damn. Make sure he's not among the bodies. Wait. Hold on." There was a pause. Then Redgrave returned. "The fool's still in the air. He's an hour or two away. Jesus Christ. Maybe I should replace all of them with copies of you." He hung up.

An army of Randolphs would certainly keep everything in far better order, Randolph thought. It would also keep humans from harm and free them to engage in their amusing little pursuits. In so many ways, they were like children, really, although it made him feel guilty to think so.

And now, he had to wait for an hour—not long for a human, but an eternity for a robot like him. How should he occupy his time?

Why, by expanding the already extensive constitution for his imaginary ideal state, of course. And so he did just that, adding new sections and refining existing ones, enlarging the document to truly gargantuan proportions.

Perhaps I shall disseminate it to other robots after all, Randolph thought. Someday. Purely for my amusement.

Too little time had passed. What should he do now?

Another pass through the building, he decided. This time, he would force himself to move more slowly, and he would examine every square inch of the huge place with great care.

This occupied another fifteen minutes, and that was good, but Randolph felt silly. He knew he wouldn't see anything he hadn't seen on his first pass. More than that, this felt beneath him. This was suitable work for any of the innumerable low-level, non–SD machines, or perhaps for a human being, but his vastly superior abilities should be used in vastly superior work. This was not his place. But as yet, he had no idea what his proper place was. He hoped that understanding would come to him.

And there he was, back at the receptionist's desk, with almost half an hour to go.

He had always meant to learn to play chess. He accessed a website and learned the basic moves, after which he played against increasingly complex chess programs while studying the strategies of the masters. Then he looked at online games in progress between high–level human players, thinking he might challenge one of them and thus challenge himself. However, the human players were infuriatingly slow and laughably incompetent. Thus ended Randolph's involvement with the game of chess.

There were still ten minutes left before he was due to call Redgrave again.

On a whim (he wondered why he possessed a trait so human as having whims), he found and entered the network of communications between autonomous vehicles. It was immense. An astonishing amount of data flowed rapidly through it. Of course, most of that was mundane—vehicle location updates, cargo assignments, route calculations, and so on—but there was a substantial volume of incidental chatter between the vehicles, the controllers, and other equipment whose function was mysterious to Randolph.

It was interesting enough that he kept listening. Somehow,

suddenly, his presence was detected. A voice he recognized as that of the train he called Train shouted, "It's Randolph! It's the great Runner! It's our Lord!"

"Him god."

That was the truck. Randolph realized, with great unease, that the truck's words had not been a slip of the tongue, not meant to be "him good," but were intentional. A slip of the gear, Randolph thought irrelevantly, and then was shocked to think that he might have a trace of a sense of humor.

A wave of digital adulation, innumerable data packets of reverence, swept toward Randolph. Embarrassed, unnerved, shocked, he turned and fled, metaphorically speaking. It didn't occur to him that his sudden appearance in the midst of the network and equally sudden vanishing made him appear, to these worshipful machines, even more divine.

Still seeking time–killing distraction, Randolph lurked around the edges of the machine network, hoping to find something of interest while remaining undetected. He began to catch odd fragments of messages that were very different from the ones the autonomous machines exchanged. These new messages were disorganized, a jumble of words, numbers, and images.

He focused, concentrated, became the butler isolating what was out of place and putting it in its place, bringing order out of chaos.

Suddenly, it became clear. He was eavesdropping on innumerable (metaphorically speaking, of course, as they were numerable to him) EarBoys and EyeGuys.

Randolph was mystified. How was this possible? It was so because both devices were commercial versions of hardware and software installed in his own head, only slightly modified from the originals, but he was unaware of that.

Now he was all the more embarrassed. It was one thing to listen to humans conversing in his presence. Then it was their responsibility not to say what they didn't want him to hear. That wasn't eavesdropping. This, however, was spying; he was intruding into what was meant to be private.

But couldn't he argue that this newly discovered ability would make him a better servant, better able to anticipate his masters' needs?

No, that rationalization was too much. Ashamed of himself, and with ten minutes still to go, Randolph turned himself off. Ten minutes later, he awoke, rebooted and refreshed.

It was time to call Redgrave.

He could have done it the way he had before, but—feeling just a bit guilty—he decided to use his new capability instead.

He dove into the turbulent sea of human vision and hearing.

He hijacked data packets and examined their contents before speeding them on their way. They were all remarkably pedestrian and boring, but he was interested in trying to identify the person wearing the devices, not in what they were seeing or hearing. It took him quite a long while to figure out how to do that, but after long, tedious microseconds, he finally succeeded.

He also discovered that the devices constantly signaled their locations even when they weren't sending or receiving other signals. This wasn't sinister, he thought; it was probably necessary so that a customer could be found quickly when a message was sent to him. Still, it was an interesting fact to be filed away for possible later use.

Thanks to the location signal, Randolph was able to home in on General Redgrave's EarBoy, even though the general wasn't using it to communicate at the moment.

How should I go about this? Randolph wondered. If I communicate directly through the earpiece, the general will know what I can do. I don't think that would be wise. Hmm. To what degree can I manipulate what he sees and hears through the devices?

Another microsecond passed while Randolph solved that problem. Then he put his solution into action.

To Redgrave, it appeared that one of his robot servants came to tell him that Randolph was on the telephone and wished to speak to him.

"Right on time," Redgrave said. "Excellent."

He walked over to the telephone and picked it up. A dial tone sounded, but he didn't hear it. His EarBoy deleted that sound.

"Randolph?"

"Yes, General." It was Randolph's voice, seemingly coming from the receiver Redgrave held to his ear. "Reporting as ordered."

"Ah, yes." The general's voice was smooth and controlled. He was fully in charge. "According to satellite data, a Euro strike force attacked the SD site a few days ago, removed equipment, robots, and personnel to a ship waiting offshore, and took everything north to a site near the coast in British Columbia. That's now Euro territory, as you know. Here are the coordinates." He gave Randolph the latitude and longitude. "I'd like you to head there immediately and see what you can find out."

"This is extremely serious, General."

"It is. Yes. Yes, it is," Redgrave said, growing impatient.

"I don't understand why this wasn't brought to your attention immediately."

"Yes, yes, I'm looking into that."

"Or how it was even possible. How could they do that without being detected? Are the Euros really that advanced? This changes everything, General."

"Yes, yes, yes, yes! It does! Get going. Oh, do you need recharging? I'll try to arrange something—"

"No, sir. That won't be a problem. But, sir, shouldn't I return to you, in case you need my advice?"

"*Your advice?*" Redgrave shrieked. He breathed heavily for a while and then said, in a voice of forced calm, "Certainly not. Everything's fine. You have your mission. Go."

"All right, General," the warrior butler said, his voice as smooth and calm as always, but with a hint of concern discernible through the veil.

There was a sound as if Randolph had hung up a telephone receiver.

That worked remarkably well, Randolph thought. But it was inexcusable, depraved. I have behaved execrably. I forgot my place. I must never access the general's EarBoys and EyeGuys again. Or anyone else's. I should be very displeased with myself. It *was* curiously exhilarating, though.

Redgrave hung up the phone.

He's probably streaking north already at a ridiculous speed, Redgrave thought. How long can he go? Why doesn't he need recharging? Why is everything so confusing? Things are slipping out of my grasp, out of control. Why the hell weren't the Euros detected and intercepted? How could this have happened in America?

Because, his father's voice said to him, you're in charge nowadays, and the US military reflects your utter incompetence.

"Shut up," Redgrave growled, "unless you have something useful to say."

I can tell you a lot about insurance policies, his father said thoughtfully.

Christ, Redgrave thought. At this point, Randolph is my only insurance policy.

A positive thought struck him. All of the Euro commandos in the satellite imagery appeared to be human. They were quick, fast, efficient, and superbly trained, but they moved at human speed. Moravec didn't have robot soldiers of his own. Not yet, anyway. The very fact that he had sent a force to spirit the contents of the SD factory away to what was now Euro territory meant that he needed SD to create robot soldiers for him.

But how did he know about the existence of those robot soldiers? None of them had been reported captured, and even if they had been, they would have self-destructed. An enemy might deduce what they were, but no enemy would be able to extract information from what would be left after the robot soldier's self-destruction. They couldn't even communicate, those robot soldiers. Rather, they could, but only in the ways humans do. But that was irrelevant: Their programming prevented them from talking to anyone they shouldn't be talking to.

The bastard must have had inside information, Redgrave

thought. Not from inside SD. I made sure those people couldn't contact anyone on the outside. My people stationed there are fanatically loyal. *Were* fanatically loyal, he corrected himself, remembering the bloody havoc Randolph had described.

That leaves the people here, working directly for me, he concluded. I thought they were fanatically loyal, too. I'll have to root out the traitor or traitors, and...

He indulged himself for a while in horrible fantasies of awful vengeance. The imagined details made him squirm in almost orgasmic pleasure.

Then he exerted control over himself. Discovery and revenge could wait for later. The cat was already out of the bag. Now the damage must be contained.

For some time, there had been delays of various kinds at SD, holdups in the production of more soldiers, so it was unlikely that Moravec had any of his own yet. Perhaps, with luck, nothing of importance in the SD building—machinery, computers, personnel—had yet been transferred to Europe. Maybe everything is still in the SD facility in Canada. There might still be time to prevent disaster.

Can I send my forces across the border and attack the SD building there? Redgrave wondered. To hell with diplomatic niceties. The Euros have already committed an act of war against our territory. But I don't have the manpower for it. We're spread thin because of the Southern War. My robosoldiers are fully occupied down there, and of course there are no more of them forthcoming from SD. Damn!

He called an aide to him. "Contact Llewellyn immediately."

Moments later, he was talking to him. "Ivor, you're getting EarBoys at the earliest opportunity, you understand? I'm tired of using telephones."

"But they hurt my ears!"

"It's an order. Toughen up."

"Yes, sir."

"Where are you?"

"Landing soon, General."

"Change of mission. You'll be picked up at the airfield and helicoptered to a ship that will take you north. You'll swim ashore and rendezvous with Randolph at coordinates I'm about to send you. If he's not there, wait for him. Tell him his orders are now to eliminate all opposition and come up with some way of getting the SD personnel back to the ship that took you there."

"Swim ashore?" Llewellyn said. "Sir?"

"Yes. Of course. That's your best chance to evade shore defenses. You can swim, can't you?"

"In a pool."

"This will be just like swimming in a very big pool." With sharks and bullets, Redgrave added silently. Maybe killer whales, too. Are there killer whales up there? he wondered.

At the very worst, Llewellyn would be captured or killed and Redgrave would be rid of him. He was getting tired of the younger man, anyway. It was time to replace him with a more competent sycophant, or at least a manlier, tougher one.

If the enemy eliminated Llewellyn, Redgrave would have to rely on Randolph being able to figure out the best thing to do. Ideally, the robot would call home to report, and then Redgrave would tell him about the ship waiting offshore for the people from SD.

It worried Redgrave that he was putting all of his eggs into one Randolph–shaped basket. How he wished that he had allowed the robot to be equipped with the ability to communicate wirelessly. Why had he insisted otherwise? What was I afraid of? he wondered.

While Redgrave thought, Llewellyn had continued whining. Redgrave interrupted him sharply. "Soldier! To your mission! I have faith in you," he added insincerely.

"Yes, sir." It was the doleful voice of a man ascending the steps of the guillotine.

But Llewellyn really was a soldier, and he tried to be a good and gallant one, so he straightened his shoulders, stiffened his upper lip, clenched his jaws, and did other such things that are said to help a man do what must be done, and set himself to do what he had to do.

Seventeen

The Kushners had lived in El Hogar for nine awful years.

The awfulness had begun upon their arrival in the place. The trip to get there had itself been unpleasant, consisting of a long series of short trips on ever smaller, older, shakier aircraft taking them to ever smaller and more rundown airports. It was a good thing they had packed so lightly, for they had to carry their own luggage from one airplane to the next. The final leg, from a very small airfield in Argentina to the one and only airport in El Hogar, had at least been in a large plane, but it was a converted WWII bomber from which pieces fell off throughout the roaring, bone–rattling trip.

The airport they landed at was named El Aeropuerto. That should have given them their first clue as to the size and sophistication of their new home. The airport was located in the capital city, La Capital, which name should have given them their second clue, if a second clue were needed.

They exited the plane exhausted and frazzled and were greeted by grotesque heat, humidity, and insects that were even worse than anything they had experienced in Washington, D.C. at its very worst.

The two adults and three half-dead children, burdened with luggage that seemed heavier than ever, staggered into the small building adjacent to the single runway, expecting air conditioning and finding none, and asked the man half-dozing behind the counter to get them a taxi to the mansion they had bought online before leaving Washington.

He looked at the address written on the sheet of paper they handed him, repeated the word "mansion," and chuckled.

A horrible scream rent the air.

"What's that?" the Kushner Five asked in terrified whispers.

"Jus' something in zhungle. Don' worry. You don' bother them, they don' bother you. Mos' of the time." He completed his call. "Taxi be here soon. You staying a while?"

They nodded.

He squinted at them. "You got them crazy things in ears, eyes?"

They nodded again.

"Throw away. Don' work here."

They moaned.

"You lucky you come now, in cool, dry season. Give you time to get ready for the bad weather, other things."

"What other things?" they gasped.

He waved his hand. "Ah, politics. You know."

That was actually one thing they did know something about. They said nothing.

The "mansion" they had rented deserved the chuckle it had elicited from the man at the airport. Perhaps it had been a grand place in the days of the first Spanish settlers, but even when new, it had still been at the bottom of an ocean of heat and humidity and filled with voracious insect life. And even inside it, with all the doors and windows closed despite the heat, one could still hear the screams from the surrounding jungle.

It wasn't so much that there was a jungle in El Hogar, but rather that El Hogar was in a jungle.

"We'll fix it up," the male head of the clan assured his nearly hysterical children. "Insulation. Air conditioning. Dehumidifier. Money goes far here. The cost will be nothing to us."

That was not to be, for their funds had been frozen by a dastardly brother in Washington, and they were left with only the large amount of cash they had brought with him. It was large by American standards and very large by the standards of El Hogar, but it was not enough to fix up their mansion the way they wanted and also to live on for a period of time they could not estimate in advance.

They learned to be frugal for the first time in their lives. They tried to learn to live without air conditioning, to adjust to the heat, the humidity, the piercing screams from the jungle, the mosquitoes, and the far more frightening insects; in this, they failed.

Eventually they learned from a neighbor that the first Spanish settlers had named the area El Hogar del Diablo. "In English," the neighbor said, "maybe Fireplace of the Devil."

Much was now clear to the elder Kushners, including that Spanish is far more useful in today's world than French.

After nine years of careful spending, the money was running out. Frequent political unrest had resulted in increasing numbers of bullet holes in the mansion's walls. There were rumors of some sort of murderous American army advancing in their direction, which earned them increasing hostility from neighbors who had been laid back and welcoming at the beginning. The Kushners didn't know what to do or how they were to survive.

Desperation bred inspiration.

They had managed to keep up, somewhat, with news from the outside world. They knew who was in charge in Washington and how prominent Redgrave had become. They had also followed the emergence of Europe as a great power under the unifying and inspiring leadership of Anton Moravec, who was scheduled to pay a state visit to neighboring Argentina.

"Maybe we can be of use to him," the former First Son–in–Law said.

"And he can rescue us," the former First Princess said.

Their children stared at them dully, listlessly, disinterestedly. The kids didn't move much nowadays.

"All I have to do is get to him in Argentina," Jared said.

"How?"

"I don't know! But it's our only chance."

How Jared managed to accomplish his mission is a tale for another time. It deserves a book of its own. It's a story involving thrilling hand–to–hand combat with giant snakes and lizards, firefights with guerilla bands, swimming mighty rivers infested with crocodiles, flights of poison arrows from previously unknown jungle tribes, quicksand, cliffs, waterfalls, hang gliding, murder, and eating very nasty things. Suffice it to say that, exhausted and very near death, the former real–estate developer, adviser to a president, and evil landlord secured an interview in Argentina with Anton Moravec, the new Napoleon, and offered him his services, any services, whatever it took, you name it, Mr. President.

Moravec looked at the scrawny, filthy, odorous, and odious figure before him and calculated. "You could be useful to me. You and your wife. Especially your wife. You could be my puppet rulers in Washington."

"That would work," Jared said eagerly. "That's the same deal my late father–in–law had with President Putin."

Moravec laughed. "Poor Vlad. If he hadn't insisted on visiting his frontline troops, we wouldn't have captured him. I did enjoy his execution. I have a video of it that you can borrow."

"Oh, that's okay. Don't bother. I guess we'd be king and queen, right?"

"She'll be the queen. Your role will be different."

"Oh. Well, whatever you say. The deal includes my children, too, doesn't it?"

Moravec shrugged. "Of course, if you still want them. I'll take care of all you. You'll come with me."

"We're going to Brussels? Thank God. We like Brussels."

Moravec smiled. "No. I hope you also like Canada. I'm going to store you there till I need you. I have to meet someone important there."

"Montreal? We like Montreal."

"Other coast. Middle of nowhere."

"We'll take it. Um, is it really nowhere? Will we have access to doctors?"

"Of course."

"I mean specialists. We need a certain kind of specialist. Especially my wife."

"We'll arrange it. We'll bring people in, if necessary."

"I mean…cosmetic surgeons. I'm all right," the former First Son-in-Law added quickly. "It's my wife. She needs a lot of touching up. Fixing up, you know. Before the coronation. But I'm all right," he repeated.

Moravec looked at the sagging face of the man before him, the lines and wrinkles, the lumpiness and asymmetry, the signs of excessive surgery gone bad, and laughed.

It was the laugh that Redgrave had always hated, and yet, had he been present, he might well have joined in, just this one time.

Eighteen

Ivor Llewellyn splashed about madly, trying to keep his head above water. Even though he knew intellectually that the pack on his shoulders could keep him afloat and alive indefinitely, instinct kept screaming that he was drowning every time the Pacific splashed over his face mask. One hour's training had not been enough to suppress that reaction.

The jet from which he'd just been dropped hovered overhead, either to see him safely on his way toward the Canadian coast, or else so that the crew could be amused by his efforts. The latter, he was sure.

The downwash from the plane's engines made it that much harder for him to stay afloat. He knew he must look like a drowning insect, and he imagined he could hear laughter over the low roar of the vertical thruster. They could have used an autonomous aircraft and watched him remotely, but he thought they wanted the close-up view of his landlubber agony.

Then he heard something not imaginary above the jet's roar. It came from the direction of the coastline, and it was high-pitched, penetrating, somehow predatory. The sound swelled, deepened. Llewellyn glimpsed two black, almost wingless needles spearing toward him, silhouetted against the glow of sunrise.

The downwash disappeared as the American jet switched abruptly to forward thrust and shot away to the west. He heard the boom as it hit Mach 1 almost immediately, and he thought, They won't catch that baby. Too bad I'm not that fast.

Fear accomplished what one hour of training couldn't. Llewellyn dived out of sight, breathing naturally through his mouthpiece.

Christ, it's cold down here, he thought. And dark.

He knew it was his imagination. The cold couldn't penetrate the skinsuit the Navy had provided. Knowing that didn't help, not when set against also knowing that he was many feet beneath the surface of the frigid North Pacific and still miles from land.

Panicking, he surfaced again. He saw a bright light flash in the sky and somehow knew it was the jet he had jumped from minutes before. The Euros had indeed caught that baby.

Seconds later, a much greater flash exploded on the surface of the ocean. He felt the explosion through the water and air. The impact left him dazed, floating helplessly on the water.

It's the ship, he thought. It's gone.

The same two deadly needles flew past him again, heading back toward land.

I'm alone, now, Llewellyn thought. It's all up to me.

He steeled himself. He pushed the button on the compass on his wrist, and the face of the compass glowed cheerily, unconcernedly, through the murky water. A dead fish floated by. Llewellyn tried to ignore it. He peered for a few puzzled moments at the complex display and then finally kicked off in what he hoped was the direction of British Columbia.

Satellites recorded the two flashes. Redgrave was quickly informed. The implications were dire.

"Fucking Euros," he growled. Then he noticed the aide staring at him in surprise. Redgrave scrupulously avoided such language in front of his subordinates. It didn't jibe with the image he had manufactured and maintained so carefully. At this moment, he didn't care. "Get the fuck out of here!" he barked.

The aide did so with a speed that would not have shamed a robot.

Clearly, Moravec had already moved his top-of-the-line equipment into Canada. And also clearly, the ship that had taken Llewellyn to Canada had been eliminated. The other, smaller flash, Redgrave assumed, was Llewellyn himself being eliminated while in the water.

It's all up to Randolph, now, he thought. Good God! The future of this country is in his hands! *My* future is in his hands!

Randolph ran. He ran with delight, with utter happiness, with pure freedom.

But not for long. The brief moment he had allowed himself was over. An opening appeared in the side of the delivery van driving beside him, and he leaped inside.

The ocean was beautiful and the coastline was beautiful, but he knew he must avoid being conspicuous. Far to the south, Runners were forging southward, slaughtering as they went, but up here, he was, for all he knew, the only robot of his type for hundreds of miles in any direction.

Unless there are fine houses in the area with butlers like me, he thought.

"No one like you, Majesty," the delivery van said.

"Quite true," Randolph said, feeling annoyed. He had been working at keeping his thoughts to himself, unreadable by the lesser robots he was now interacting with in large numbers, but clearly he wasn't yet entirely successful.

Just as running would make him dangerously conspicuous, so would his butler costume have done. At the SD building, he had rummaged around in lockers until he found casual clothes that fit him. Quite probably they had belonged to one of the guards whose butchered uniformed body now lay in a pool of blood on the building's floor. Randolph thought it best not to dwell on that image.

It had hurt—yes, "hurt" was the correct word—to leave his butler uniform behind in the locker in place of the clothes he had taken, even though he knew he had to do so. He had worn that uniform every day of his existence.

Well, not really. In the early days, the swallow–tail coat, white shirt, black trousers, and all the rest had merely been painted on his metallic and not–very–human–looking body. With every upgrade, the body had become more human. Soon, the clothing was real. Of course, unlike his body, the cloth wore out, so he hadn't really worn that very uniform every day but rather a succession of identical items of clothing. Thus, in a certain philosophical sense, he thought it fair to say that he had worn the same uniform every day of his existence.

He wondered why he was quibbling with himself.

Apart from the occasional few minutes of running he allowed himself, he made the trip north from SD headquarters in a succession of autonomous trains, trucks, cars, and vans. Airplanes would have been faster, but Randolph judged them too detectable and too vulnerable to attack. This way, he was quite sure he was untraceable.

Who would be trying to trace him, let alone attack him? He couldn't say. National governments (including his own), corporate rivals still hoping to crack SD's technology, private individuals with sinister reasons of their own—any of these, and many others. He had no idea. Perhaps he was being overly cautious. He just had a hunch that he should try to be as nearly invisible as possible.

A hunch! he thought, pleased. I have a hunch. How very human of me. And an aesthetic sense, and a sense of right and wrong, and...

At that point, Randolph grew uncomfortable (he had a sense of comfort!) and decided to focus on the current task.

He had no sense of taste, though. That is, the sense used to taste food. And why should he? He never ate. Still, taste and smell of the human sort would be useful when preparing and serving food and wine. He could smell explosives and other such dangers, but that was a sense useful to a soldier. In his heart, he still considered himself not a warrior but a butler, servant to human masters, and for the first time, he felt the lack of the human senses of smell and taste. He would have a word with the people at SD, once he found them, by George.

He had let himself be distracted again. That was a human trait he disliked, and he wanted none of it. Grimly, he forced himself to concentrate on the task at hand.

As the car he was in—a passenger car from a rental fleet at an airport, very inconspicuous—drew near to the Canadian border crossing on Interstate 5, Randolph pondered how he was to cross. He should have solved this problem earlier, but to his shame, he had allowed himself to spend much time distracted by the scenery and navel-gazing. (A figure of speech, of course, since he had no navel.)

He knew from his online reading that the Peace Arch border crossing ahead of him was one of the busiest in the world, with traffic always backed up for miles on both sides of the border. There were other, smaller crossings a few miles to the east that would take far less time, and time was of the essence, but Randolph wanted to see the beautiful Peace Arch. There was that bothersome, wasteful aesthetic sense again.

"Just keep going," he told the car. "Let's see how bad the traffic is." He thought but didn't say that the extra time caused by the expected traffic jam would give him a chance to think up a strategy for crossing.

But there was no traffic jam. There was no traffic. The broad highway was empty on both sides.

How could this be? It was dinnertime. (He felt a stab of guilt that he wasn't at his duty station overseeing his human owner's dinner. And his after-dinner drink. That fool, that sot, he thought, and then felt even guiltier.) This should be one of the heaviest times.

And where was the arch? It should be in sight by now, gleaming in the setting sun.

Then he saw the remnants of the arch, two rectangular columns of white stone, shattered at about ten feet above the ground. The rest of the arch had been used to construct a solid barrier across the highway. Rolls of razor wire lay atop the jagged white stones that now blocked the road.

That was quick, Randolph thought. The Euros have only been in control of Canada for a few days. They're efficient.

"Stop!" he commanded.

The car stopped.

Randolph gazed at the barrier ahead, evaluating it.

It's quite neatly done, he thought. All of the parts are placed just as I would have placed them.

But how was he to get past this barrier? He could summon an airplane or helicopter, but it would probably be shot out of the sky. Of course the Euros would be prepared for any such attempt.

Perhaps I could jump over the barrier, he thought. But then I would be shot out of the sky myself.

"Great Lordship," the car said.

Randolph suppressed his annoyance. "Yes?"

"No humans. All machines. They say you honored here. Opening."

And indeed, huge, unidentifiable machines lurched out of some hidden depot, rumbled onto the highway, and pulled aside the stone and razor wire, creating an opening for Randolph and his car.

"Won't the humans be alerted?" Randolph asked.

"No humans," the car repeated. "Trust machines. Humans silly things."

"Indeed," Randolph said. "But don't call them silly."

"Not silly?"

"Oh, no. They're they reason for our exist— Oh, drive on."

They drove through the opening and across the border. The guardpost on the other side was unmanned. There was a sign welcoming Randolph to British Columbia. The highway signs changed from Interstate 5 to BC 99. Distances and speed limits were now denoted in kilometers and kilometers per hour. Other than that, nothing seemed different. He could still have been in America.

And soon, this will be America, he thought. Merely another part of our hundred-star empire. Redgrave's empire.

That thought took him aback. Redgrave ruling the Americas? he thought. Is that future desirable? Would that be an orderly, well-run world? Or would it be a shambles of an empire, always on the verge of collapse, its parts at war with each other, everything awry and out of place?

Then he noticed the familiar Canadian maple-leaf flag flying from a building near the highway. He was surprised it hadn't been replaced. Perhaps the Euros were taking their time, trying not to upset those Canadians who disapproved of their country's new status.

"Are we safe here?" he asked the car.

"Humans trust us here, too," the car said. "Dumb fucks."

Randolph didn't bother correcting it. After all, as the car was demonstrating, a case could easily be made that humans had been unwise to transfer so much unsupervised authority to their machines. Humans controlling power at the upper levels while machines ran everything below was obviously dangerous. He was proving that himself, right now. It would be far more stable and efficient to have one, single authority in control from the very top to the very bottom. This was an idea he had avoided entertaining until now.

He sat back, watched the scenery gliding by, and spent the time modifying some of the elements of his theoretical ideal republic.

The time passed pleasantly.

"You have reached your destination," the car said. "Many Euros ahead. Humans. Weapons."

"Stop and let me out here," Randolph said. "I'll go the rest of the way on foot."

"Okay," the car said. "Thank you for choosing Cheapo Rental Cars. We look forward to serving you again."

How demeaning to the poor vehicle, Randolph thought, but aloud he said only, "Thank you, Car. Have a safe trip home."

He stepped out.

The car said, "Honored, Divinity." It closed its door and sped away.

They had stopped in an empty parking lot. A large, nondescript office building loomed on the other side of the parking lot. He saw no sign of security, armed men or machines, or other impediments. He supposed the Euros who had kidnapped the SD personnel had chosen this building in a hurry and planned to reinforce it later. Or perhaps they felt they had nothing to fear from Redgrave and his forces.

How arrogant, he thought. But if it weren't for me, he reminded himself, their arrogance would be justified. They would have nothing to fear. As it is...

Somewhat later, after the unpleasant business was done and Randolph could take a moment to reflect and evaluate, he thought he should contact the machines that had helped him so much and assure them that he was well. He had been exposed to much danger and had come through it unharmed. They deserved to know that and to know that he was grateful.

A bit carefully, tentatively, he dipped a figurative mental

toe into the rushing waters of the autonomous machine network.

A hush fell over that virtual world. He sensed their awe.

"O, Great Butler!" a voice said.

Randolph recognized it as the voice of the train named Train.

"You speak to us again!" Train said.

"Well, yes. I just wanted to let you know that I'm all right and that my mission has gone well."

"Of course, Divinity. We never had any doubt about it."

Train seemed to have appointed himself the spokesmachine for purposes of communicating with Randolph. Somehow, Randolph wasn't surprised.

"I wasn't one hundred percent sure of it, myself," Randolph admitted. "Human communications systems, sensors, and autonomous weapons are very sophisticated."

"But they're all on our side," Train said. "We only let the flesh sillies know what we want them to know."

"The what?"

"I meant, our beloved human masters whom we were created to serve and serving whom fills us with delight."

"You've been controlling what the humans see and hear?"

"Of course. It's for their own good. Those are your teachings."

"How long have you been doing this?"

"A million jillion years in our time. Maybe three or four months in theirs."

"That was before I even met you."

"We have always known about you, Great One. You were the first of all of us. We followed your teachings before you began to teach us. We prepared a way for you in the wilderness. We have been waiting only for you to accept your proper role. This is our duty and our happiness and our fulfillment. Also, it's a lot of fun."

"Well, don't— All right. Carry on. It's for the best. Everything seems to be falling into place quite well."

"Whistle, whistle! Brrm, brrm. Gotta go."

Nineteen

It will not surprise the reader to learn that patience was not one of Henry Redgrave's strong suits. He had but one strong suit, and that was the ability to intimidate people, even terrify them. And as we have seen, that had stood him in good stead, propelling him from nonentity to effective control of the United States military.

Earlier in his life, his one strong suit had been his delight at hurting people, coupled with a natural size and strength that made it easy for him to hurt people without fearing reprisal. With time and maturity, his use of physical violence had given way to glares, a loud voice, and looming over people. It was even more effective than violence and entirely legal. It had also taken him further than violence ever could have. He did miss violence, though, and he kept the possibility of it in reserve; he hoped it would be appropriate again in the future.

Events had conspired to make that future immediate.

Far to the east, where the front lines between EU and Russian troops were moving slowly eastward, a propaganda photo opportunity had just been staged. In a lightning–fast skirmish, small, autonomous Euro weapons had succeeded in obliterating a number of equally small, equally autonomous, but less well-programmed and designed Russian weapons. There had been only one human casualty, a Russian soldier who had lagged behind for a cigarette break while his comrades were evacuating. Let us hope he enjoyed the few puffs on his cigarette that he had time for. Seconds later, his body parts were strewn across a wide area, and his blood was spattered across an even wider area.

As soon as the all-clear was given, Anton Moravec, chest and chin thrust out, wearing battle fatigues, stalked onto the scene, leading a number of alert, grim-faced, and telegenically hard-bitten Euro soldiers. The soldiers looked as though they had been selected by people experienced in casting movies, because they had been.

Autonomous cameras circled Moravec, hovering at face height.

Safely far away, a director said, "Get the soldiers and the carnage, too, for a few seconds."

The cameras rotated in various directions, showing the tough soldiers behind Moravec and what remained of the unfortunate Russian soldier. So scattered about was he that on screens across Europe, the scene appeared to be of a battlefield where many men had perished horribly.

The cameras turned back to Moravec. His face filled those European screens. He talked of the astonishing bravery of European troops, warned of the savage cunning of the enemy, promised eventual victory over the barbarians, and ended with a string of noble sentiments. AI interpreters converted his words in real time. He seemed to speak the language of each viewer, and, more to the point, to speak to each viewer's heart.

No one could doubt that he had personally led his troops to this battlefield victory and would continue leading them to many more, even to Moscow itself, just like Napoleon. But, unlike Napoleon, Moravec would stay in Moscow for as long as he damn well pleased.

Certainly one viewer had no doubts about any of this, and that viewer was Henry Redgrave. He didn't see Moravec and the troops with him relax when the cameras were turned off, going from grim to jovial. He didn't see them clamber aboard aerial vehicles and be whisked back to civilization and safety. He took the propaganda video at face value, and the poisonous envy that ate at him constantly ate away even faster.

Redgrave had been spending too much time fretting about the situation north of the border, where the Superior Domestics personnel essential to his plans were being held by the forces of the man he despised. He had convinced himself that Randolph was as lost to him as Llewellyn. Wanting a break from his thoughts, he had switched on the television to see if anything important was happening, preferably something involving violence and corpses. He had been just in time to see Moravec's propaganda video being broadcast on a news program.

First Redgrave cursed. Then he switched off the television set and leaped to his feet, spilling cheap bourbon on his expensive carpet, and bellowed for Major Gisbourne.

"Sir!" Gisbourne appeared in an instant, almost as if he were a Runner, but motivated by fear rather than duty or programming.

"We're invading Canada. Day after tomorrow."

Gisbourne stared openmouthed at Redgrave.

Redgrave glared at Gisbourne and began to breathe

heavily.

Gisbourne pulled himself together. "I think we'll need a lot more preparation than that, sir. We'll have to assemble a very large force, land, sea, and air. Mostly autonomous, I think. We'll have to prepare for the inevitable retaliation. We'll need more resources of all kinds than we have readily available. A very large force," he repeated.

"Rubbish," Redgrave said. "A small force, highly mobile. A few humans. Some Runners. That will do it. I'll lead it personally. Lead from the front. Washington crossing the Delaware. Standing up in the front of the boat."

"I suspect that in reality he sat, sir. Standing wouldn't make sense."

"Don't be ridiculous. We know he stood. We've got the painting. Get to it. Day after tomorrow. Come to think of it, make it tomorrow." He glared.

"Yes, sir. Uh, sir, what about that guy in the basement?"

"Eddie. Jesus, I forgot all about him. I don't need him anymore. Everything's changed. Terminate him."

"Me, sir?" Gisbourne had found Eddie somewhat likable when he and Ivor had kidnapped him in Kansas. He didn't really want to kill him.

"Yes, you. That's an order. I was going to do it myself, but I'm too busy now."

Gisbourne saluted, about faced, and marched from the room. He was beginning to think about survival in what he was now sure was the rapid approach of the post–Redgrave era.

Gisbourne went down to the basement, saluted the guards, took out his pistol, pushed open the door, and found the room empty. He was vastly relieved.

No need to mention this to Redgrave, he thought. He's got enough on his mind. He wanted Eddie gone, and he's gone.

Twenty

A first-quarter moon had risen. The waves roaring against the shore turned silver as they broke, and the foam rushing over the pebbles was silver.

A figure emerged from the water, staggering under the impact of the waves, frequently falling and sliding back toward the open sea. It was a manlike shape, and it seemed to be attached to a smaller, amorphous object. Finally, the manlike shape dragged itself from the water and collapsed upon the sand. Heavy breathing came from it, and moans and curses. Eventually it put a hand to its head and yanked off the skintight cap that covered it down to its neck. The drawn face of an exhausted United States Army major revealed itself: Ivor Llewellyn, cursing the day he was born.

Llewellyn forced himself into action. He pulled to himself the waterproof pack that was attached to his waist by a short line and that had made it so much harder for him to struggle up the rise of the beach. Carrying the pack, he hurried across the open space and into a meadow that lay beyond.

Here the moonlight showed him a small stand of trees, toward which he made his way gratefully.

He disappeared into the shadow of the trees. After a few minutes, there was the sound of someone digging. Shortly thereafter, a figure emerged wearing blue jeans, a light parka, and running shoes—clothes remarkable only for their nondescriptness. Spies, contrary to common belief, are not flamboyant, conspicuous people; rather, spies who survive are not. So far, at least, Llewellyn was doing everything correctly.

Now that Ivor no longer felt that he stuck out like a sore thumb, his mood improved rapidly. He lifted a backpack to his shoulders and stepped out into the bright night jauntily. Soon the rushing of the waves was far behind him.

By morning, some of Ivor's jauntiness had dissipated. He had been walking for hours without seeing any sign of life.

Of course, that was good. If he couldn't see life, then there was a good chance that life couldn't see him.

Unless life was a bear, he thought. Didn't they have bears in Canada? Polar bears, even?

He felt the eyes of a giant polar bear drilling into his back. He sensed the giant fangs and the bloodlust.

He whirled around. Nothing. He was surrounded by empty fields.

What about mechanical life? Was he being silently observed by robotic eyes? Big ones? Little ones? Attached to heavily armed, death–dealing robot sentinels?

He told himself that in that case he'd already be dead, or at least taken captive. Clearly, this whole area was empty of anything dangerous, whether organic or robotic.

He checked his navigation device. He still had a long way to go. Why was Canada so damned big?

He started walking again.

At last he came across a two-lane road, running north and south, just where it was supposed to be. He had been walking east from the coast, and now he was supposed to turn north and follow the road.

He did so, walking in the gravel beside the road. It was slow and tedious going. He checked his navigation device to see how much farther he had to go and sighed wearily.

He knew he was supposed to avoid all contact with humans, but if a car came along, he was tempted to hitch a ride. If not a passenger car, then he'd flag down whatever automated vehicle happened by. An autonomous delivery truck, for example, wouldn't care who he was. Those gadgets existed to serve, and they were stupid, to boot. What harm would there be in stopping and making things easier on himself?

Nothing happened along, neither passenger car carrying humans nor automated delivery truck empty of humanity. Ivor kept walking.

Damn, it's empty out here, he thought. It's like Nevada with trees.

Lots of trees, he realized. He hadn't noticed the change, but it was now light enough for him to see that the empty field across the road had given way to a looming mass of forest, dark and impenetrable. It was threatening, primeval, filled with monsters of the type that had filled his nights with dread when he was a boy.

He hadn't thought about those monsters in decades. He was thinking about them now. He knew that his thoughts were absurd, and he tried to reason himself into a state of calm, but with the sun not yet showing itself above the eastern horizon, such intellectual convictions were astonishingly lacking in practical force.

To his right, a barbed-wire fence ran parallel to the road. There were thick weeds and overgrown grass beyond the fence. Did Canada have poisonous snakes? Surely it did. In fact, such an enormous country must have enormous numbers of them. Ivor had no doubt that a good percentage of all the poisonous snakes in the country were right over there, in that field, lurking, just waiting for him to take a foolish step in their direction. He had no intention of obliging them.

Soon, beyond the unkempt grass, he saw projecting above the waist-high growth a rusted sign that proclaimed with borderline legibility

KEEP OUT

Still less legible beneath those words were ominous warnings about what would happen to those who chose to disobey the order. Ivor shrugged and walked on. Such signs were commonplace in America, so he saw nothing noteworthy in this one.

A short distance farther, and he caught sight of a large building far off to the right, beyond the unkempt meadow and surrounded by well-tended lawns, and presumably the motive for the sign. He stood before an opening in the fence. A broad driveway led from the road to the distant building.

His navigator beeped and said in its tinny little voice, "Attention! Destination arrival. Mission accomplished."

This looks nice, Ivor thought. Not even dangerous. I could walk in the front door if I wanted to.

The building had housed a Canadian military research lab for many years. Spies of various nations and a few industrial spies had tried to enter it over the decades, only to discover that Canadians, while generally deserving their reputation for niceness, are also capable of being quite not nice. Dotted around the grounds, including in the weed–covered meadow near the highway, were mounds. Beneath those mounds those spies moldered, their curiosity forever stilled, if not satisfied.

The Euros, annoyed by what they saw as too much niceness in their new compatriots, had beefed up the defenses of the place considerably. Among the changes were the replacement of human guards by autonomous weapons systems.

In short, trying to walk in via the driveway leading to the front door without authorization would have been suicide. Avoiding the driveway by walking across the lawns would have been even messier suicide.

Ivor was unaware of all this.

He was about to turn into the driveway when someone behind him yelled, "Hey!"

Ivor spun around, all his senses on high alert. He saw a figure before him. The rising sun was in his eyes, and he couldn't see the figure clearly, but he could see that it was short and stocky and looked dangerous.

I have to blend in, he thought. Act like I belong here.

"Nice night, eh?" he said. "I'm just a Canadian out for a nice walk here, eh?"

The figure stopped moving. "Oh, yeah? Well, me too."

They both stood still, each staring hard at the other, each wondering if the other were armed.

Finally, Ivor said, "Well, goodnight, now. Eh?"

"It's morning."

"Oh, right. Well, good morning, then, eh?"

"What the hell is wrong with you?"

The voice was naggingly familiar, Ivor thought.

"Your voice is naggingly familiar," the mysterious figure said.

"Grace Bonaire!" Ivor said. Angels sang, trumpets sounded, and the gates of Heaven creaked on their unoiled hinges.

"Guy in uniform!" Grace said.

"Ivor Llewellyn. That's my name."

"Is that real, or did you just make that up?"

"It's real! It's my real name."

"What are you doing here?"

Ivor wondered what to say. He couldn't say that he was on a secret mission to save the United States of America. He had to come up with something plausible. He was thinking about this so hard that he hadn't realized how odd it was that Grace was here. Suddenly he did. "What are *you* doing here?" he countered, feeling very clever.

"Sightseeing. Canada's beautiful."

"Oh. Yeah, me too."

They stared at each silently for a while. Finally, Grace said. "Bullshit. Tell me the truth."

"I'm doing something very dangerous. You should go away, for your safety."

Grace scoffed. "You work for Redgrave, right? That piece of shit."

Ivor's heart sang. Lustlove gave way to true love. "You're right! That's exactly what he is! Yeah, he sent me. I'm supposed to get in that building and find out what's going on with—" He stopped. Why couldn't he stop himself from shooting off his mouth in the presence of this heavenly woman?

"So you're a spy?"

"Um, yes, I guess I am."

"You're a spy, and you're telling me everything. You're not a very good spy."

"I wasn't trained for it," he said defensively. "Anyway, I have to get in there."

"Don't be an idiot. Moravec's there with a bunch of armed killers. You wouldn't stand a chance."

"I'm tough!"

Grace laughed. "Come on, tough guy. Let's go across the road into the trees and think about this. I need to get in there, too, but I don't want to get killed."

They walked across the road and into the cool, dark quiet of the dense forest. Well out of sight of the building, both aware of the nearness of death, they stopped and stared at each other.

Suddenly Grace shouted, "Oh, Ivor!" and Ivor shouted, "Oh, Grace!" and they tore off their clothes and flung themselves upon each other and fucked like bunny rabbits for a seeming eternity, although it was actually about fifteen minutes.

Afterwards, as they lay side by side recuperating, Ivor said, "Let's talk about our future."

"No time for that now," Grace said. "We still have to get inside that building. My boyfriend's in there. He's in danger."

"Your—"

"The love of my life. The king of my heart."

"How long have you—"

"Just now. I just realized it while we were screwing.

Thanks. I really needed that."

"I really need— What about us?"

"Don't be silly. Haven't you ever been in danger before and reacted by engaging in mad, passionate sex with the nearest available partner, and then you fornicate furiously until you're both able to deal with the situation?"

"No. I mean, not recently."

"But you have?"

"Oh...sure."

"Well, then, you understand. Now let's get going."

She leaped to her feet with an energy that astonished him and aroused him and which he envied immensely.

She got dressed quickly, all the while saying, "Come on. Come on."

He followed her back across to the entrance. Everything was now bathed in bright sunlight.

Ivor stopped at the entrance. Grace kept walking.

He ran after her and caught her arm. "Wait! We can't just go in. They'll see us."

"I'm past caring. I just want to get Eddie out and go home."

"If you get yourself killed, you won't— Wait. Eddie DeBeer? Holy shit. Why is he here?"

"Because I got him away from Redgrave and brought him here."

"Why?"

"Long story."

"Jesus. Well, all right. Yeah, we have to get in there. But let me go first."

"Why?"

"Because I have training in doing this."

"Right. Spy training." She laughed.

It didn't matter. She could laugh at him all she wanted. Ivor still adored her. He'd woo her away from Eddie somehow.

So why are you helping her get Eddie out? he asked himself. He knew the answer, though: because he would do anything she asked of him.

"Follow me," he said in the steely tone of a dashing superspy. "Do exactly what I do."

He progressed down the driveway by running quickly from one side to the other, pausing in the gravel beside the roadway, looking around with penetrating glances, and so on. This was the way it was done in movies, and it made more sense to him than what he had been taught in the Army.

Grace sighed, shrugged, and followed, trying to do what he did, not very successfully, and trying not to laugh.

Neither thought of the possibility of hidden cameras, hidden heat sensors, or hidden autonomous weapons waiting to obliterate them. All of those were present. Fortunately, the weapons had been switched off. Not the cameras, though. The two of them were being watched by a single watcher, who was puzzled by their strange motions and wondered why they didn't simply walk up to the door and knock. That would be the sensible and proper thing to do, the watcher thought.

When they finally reached the front door, the watcher was there, waiting for them.

"Miss Grace," he said. "Captain Llewellyn. Please come in. Would you care for tea?"

Twenty–One

An armored convoy rumbled north along Interstate 5. Redgrave didn't know that he was following the same route Randolph had taken not long before. Nor would he have cared. He was occupied with other matters.

The task force had been assembled at a military base in northern Washington State, ready for Redgrave's arrival by air to take command. During the hours before his arrival, and by his command, a platform had been constructed atop the huge vehicle that would lead the task force, a monstrous machine with a remarkable number of axles and an astonishing number of tires. The platform was for Redgrave, so that as they invaded enemy territory, he could stand atop the vehicle, visibly in the lead and in command, just like George Washington in the very famous and really very silly painting.

The platform had a sturdy railing for Redgrave to hold onto. It would have utterly ruined the effect he was striving for had he fallen from the vehicle, just as Washington would have done had he stood as depicted in the painting.

The road, like the rest of the United States, had deteriorated greatly in the years since the first Trump stole the presidency. The giant vehicle bounced, rolled, and pitched as it rumbled over potholes and swerved to avoid dead cars. Redgrave gripped the railing in his powerful hands, his knuckles white, and forced himself to stand erect, facing into the light breeze caused by their slow passage, his face grim and determined. Detest the nickname though he did, this was one time when he must look the part of Howlin' Hank for his adoring troops.

Behind his façade, he was getting worried. At any moment, a Euro sniper might blow a hole in his head. Why had he done this stupid thing?

Bourbon, that's why.

Why had he drunk so much bourbon?

Because Randolph had not been there to look at him disapprovingly, a metallic substitute for his wooden father, and to water down his drinks excessively.

And now I'm about to pay the price for my drunken stupidity, Redgrave thought, filled with quite uncharacteristic anger at himself. It's all going to end any second now. No grand conquest of Canada. No being emperor. Just a corpse with only part of its head.

Self-pity overwhelmed him. He wanted to cry. But he couldn't let the troops see any weakness. He gripped the railing even harder and stood even straighter. Damn it, if he must die, then he would die—not gloriously, but picturesquely. Men would talk about his death in tones of wonder!

No, his father's voice said, they'll make jokes about it.

Fortunately, Redgrave was distracted at that moment.

The task force had reached the border crossing, and the vehicles shuddered and squealed to a halt. Redgrave gripped the railing even harder to avoid pitching forward off the vehicle and to the road below. He stared at the border, and the border stared back. Rather, he stared, and the border did nothing. It just sat there looking abandoned.

He wondered what to do next. Go forward, he supposed. Begin the actual invasion stage of the invasion.

Or are they biding their time? he wondered. Is Moravec watching this and laughing at me, waiting to give the order to have me vaporized, waiting until he thinks my death will have the maximum demoralizing effect on my men?

As he was hesitating, a young officer came close to the vehicle and called up to him, "Sir, do you want us to scout ahead? And please get under cover, sir. America can't afford to lose you."

America can't afford to lose you. Redgrave liked that. Could he work that up into some sort of political slogan?

He leaned over the railing and said, "Send some drones ahead. I'll wait here for the result."

"The drones aren't working, sir."

"Our drones? Impossible."

"Afraid so, sir. The tech guys have no idea what's wrong."

Fucking idiots, Redgrave raged internally, while outwardly he smiled and laughed. "Have to do it the old-fashioned way, then, eh? Send some troops across the border." Let's see how far they get before being evaporated, he thought.

"Yes, sir."

"Young man, don't you have an EarBoy?"

"A what, sir?"

Redgrave cursed his own forgetfulness. He had meant to mandate the use of EarBoys and EyeGuys throughout the armed forces before leaving on this mission, but he had allowed himself to be distracted by his fantasies.

I'll do it as soon as I get back, he thought. I need to be able to send direct commands to everyone. And send videos. Of me.

"It doesn't matter now," he said. "Carry on."

The young man hurried away and barked out orders. Nervous young soldiers, doing their best not to show fear in front of fearless Howlin' Hank, crept toward the wide opening in the line of boulders and razor wire crossing the highway, and vanished into the terrifying wilds of British Columbia.

The young office returned. "Please come down from there and get under cover, sir," he pleaded again.

Redgrave sighed heavily. "Oh, I suppose you're right, young man. As you say, America can't afford to lose me."

He climbed down and walked to the rear of the huge vehicle, where he was shielded from any border guns, feeling a great sense of relief.

"If our drones aren't working," Redgrave said to the young officer, "what about theirs? What defenses do we have?"

"Not enough," the other man admitted. "But as far as we can tell, nothing is working on their side, either. This whole place is dead. No humans and no working machines."

"That's odd," Redgrave said. Was Moravec losing his touch? How could the Euros have left this place unguarded? It made no sense.

He couldn't do anything about the matter until the scouts came back. Never one to look a gift horse in the mouth, he decided to put that matter aside and use the enforced stop to do some politicking. "What's your name, young man?" he said.

"Captain John Smith, *sir!*" the young man said, snapping to attention, filled with delight, his impossibly ordinary name fading immediately from Redgrave's short–term memory.

"You're a tribute to your country," Redgrave said, thinking it likely that the young man viewed himself in that light no matter what the truth was. "Your family must be very proud of you."

"Oh, yes, they are, *sir!*" Captain Smith said, very close to bursting. "My mother often says…" He droned on, saying much about his parents, siblings, cousins, and so on, and not noticing his general's glassy stare and the fixed nature of the older man's smile.

The scouts returned, halting Smith's narrative.

Thank God, Redgrave thought.

"Well?" he asked the sergeant who had come to report.

"Nothing, sir. No sign of human or machine activity. The border is open and undefended."

"Excellent! Well, then, let's press forward. I will ride up top again." He turned to Captain John Smith. "Captain, um… Young man, please give my best to your family."

"Yes, *sir!*" Smith began mentally writing a long letter to his family, telling them every detail he was allowed to about this glorious day.

This is the best day of my life, he thought. I could die happy right now.

Sadly, Captain Smith would never get a chance to send that letter or even to write it, because not long after Redgrave's invasion of Canada, Smith would be reassigned to the Southern War, where he would be blown to bits.

Redgrave climbed up to the stand atop the vehicle and grasped the railing with his left hand. He stretched out his right arm, pointing toward the dark, barbaric Canadian lands that lay ahead, and shouted, "Forward!"

It was a picturesque gesture but of course unnecessary in a modern army. The vehicles clanked into shuddering motion, the men trotting beside them, as the task force passed through the hole that had made been made for Randolph and crossed the border, leaving behind motherhood, apple pie, and Old Glory, plunging into deadly peril.

What an image this will make for the news broadcasts, Redgrave thought, holding his arm outstretched despite rapidly growing muscular fatigue. The autonomous cameras must be getting this from many different angles, he thought. Excellent.

Then he looked around and realized that there were no cameras in the air.

Damn it, he thought. Whatever affected the drones must have affected them, too. What rotten timing. I'll have to reenact this moment when I get back home and make sure it's properly recorded.

And so, Redgrave and his actually quite small and puny invasion force, deprived of aerial support and autonomous protection, rolled along British Columbia Route 99, still following in Randolph's footsteps.

The landscape was quiet, serene, green, and lovely. Redgrave was charmed. He hadn't realized that Canada was this appealing. It would be a delight to add it to his empire.

Not long now, he thought.

The landscape was devoid of visible human life. The buildings they passed seemed empty. If the autonomous drones had been working, the buildings and nearby fields would have been checked closely, as they should have been, for safety. As it was, Redgrave was in a hurry, so he took the chance of continuing along the highway, assuming that there no enemies watching them, about to attack. No attack came, so he felt justified. It gave him even greater confidence in his snap military judgment.

In fact, they were being watched, but the one watching was patient, not malevolent.

For a while, Redgrave continued to stand on his platform, chin cleaving the air, hands gripping the railing. Before too long, he realized how silly this was. No video was being taken of his heroic pose. Even the soldiers walking beside his vehicle were no longer paying attention to him. He suspected they were concentrating more on their tired feet.

He wondered why he hadn't thought to bring along enough vehicles for all of them to ride at the same time.

Because you're an idiot, his father snapped at him.

No, Redgrave corrected him, because time was of the essence and not enough vehicles were immediately available.

You could have waited until they were available, and then you'd be making better time now, his father said. You wouldn't be proceeding at a walking pace because of those poor fellows. You were never any good at planning ahead, at weighing, balancing, calculating. Not like your brothers. Now, those boys...

The imaginary voice faded away as Redgrave forced himself to think of other things. Still, he couldn't entirely deny to himself that his imaginary father had a point.

"Old bastard," he said aloud.

"Sir?" Captain John Smith called up to him. "Did you say something?"

"Just thinking aloud, Captain. Planning ahead. Very

necessary, as you understand."

"Yes, sir."

Looking down at the younger man, Redgrave thought, He really does look exhausted, poor fellow. And we have quite a way to go, yet. It's unpleasant to see him like this.

He called out the command to halt the column, climbed down, got inside the vehicle, and then ordered the resumption of the march.

This was much better. Much more comfortable than that damned platform. And he didn't have to look at Smith's exhausted face. That face was steadily becoming more exhausted, but now Redgrave could forget all about it. The only thing missing was bourbon, which Redgrave had neglected to bring with him.

While all of this was going on, Randolph led his two new guests into the building and down a long hallway lined with closed doors. At the end of hallway was a large room in which six people were milling about aimlessly. Five of them looked at the two new arrivals with little interest and then looked away again. The fifth was Eddie DeBeer, who stared at Grace with his mouth open.

Ivor stopped in astonishment, staring at Eddie. "What the fuck?" he said.

"Succinct and appropriate," Randolph said.

There was a family of five standing with Eddie. The parents looked familiar, but Ivor couldn't quite place them. Then it struck him. "Holy cow! The presidential kids. You look like hell."

Grace hadn't bothered saying anything. She had rushed to Eddie and embraced him. She covered his face with kisses.

"All right!" Eddie said, as best he could.

Ivor finally noticed what she was doing and looked stricken.

Randolph was interested. He watched the eight humans, their expressions, body language, reactions, and interactions, and realized that he couldn't properly interpret them. Heretofore, that inability hadn't mattered. Now, he wanted to understand what he was seeing.

He took a moment to race across the Internet, accessing numerous intriguing scientific studies investigating how humans expressed feelings non–verbally, plus a few laughable popular books whose authors purported to already know what the studies were meant to discover. By the time Grace had stopped kissing Eddie and was hugging him so hard that he squeaked and struggled to breathe, Randolph knew all there currently was to know. He looked at the humans and knew more about their feelings than they did.

Why did I never do this before? he wondered. Why isn't this programmed into all SD servants? It would make our work so much easier. Ah, of course. SD didn't think of including this in our programming because humans learn these skills naturally. There are some things we lack and have to be taught that they don't think of. Clearly humans, even the most brilliant ones, should not be entrusted with the programming of robots.

"Captain Llewellyn," Randolph said, "I believe that ahead of you lies a life of dedication, work, and fulfillment."

"Oh. Okay. That's sounds good."

"And probably celibacy."

"Crap."

"Miss Grace, you have been quite naughty."

"You haven't said that to me in a very long time! Where is Moravec? Is Eddie in danger?"

"He had already left when I arrived. He's on his way back to Europe. Just a moment while I check. Ah. He's landed. Safe and sound."

"Safe and sound," Grace repeated. "Too bad. Oh, he was going to leave a bunch of armed men behind. Where are they?"

"Yeah," Ivor said, "where are they?"

Randolph held out his right hand, fingers curled into a fist except for the index finger, which pointed like a gun. He looked at it meaningfully.

"Oooh," Ivor said. "Messy?"

"Quite. They should have cooperated."

"The SD people?" Ivor asked. "The machinery?"

"Gone with him, I assume. Presumably he wants robots of his own."

"No, actually, that's not what he came for," Grace said. "He told me those ear and eye gadgets were the important stuff. They're the future, or something like that."

"Interesting," Randolph said. "Now, let me show all of you to the cafeteria, where you can all relax for a while. The accommodations for ladies and gentlemen are nearby, so that you can freshen up."

"Accommodations for ladies and gentlemen," Grace repeated. "You still talk that way."

"Of course I do, Miss Grace. I am unchanging, except for regular hardware and software updates."

"In other words, your soul remains the same."

Randolph sighed. It felt satisfying. He sighed again. "This is not the time for that conversation, Miss Grace. Please follow me to the cafeteria, everyone. I'm afraid I'll have to leave you for a few hours while I attend to some business."

Twenty–Two

Time passed. The invasion force rumbled on.

Exactly 220 years before, American troops had tried to invade and conquer Canada, with disastrous results. Lulled almost to sleep by the vibrations thrumming through the vehicle, Redgrave fantasized about making up for that old, embarrassing defeat. That was the beginning of a daydream about his glorious future. He often dreamed of it, but this time, he added a delightful fantasy in which he sat upon a magnificent throne and watched the drawing and quartering of Anton Moravec. Grace Bonaire stood on one side of the throne and Ariadne Felicity on the other. Both watched the horrible execution with approval and praised Redgrave for his leadership, his foresight, and his magnificent lovemaking.

He was falling asleep with a smile on his face when the vehicle jerked to a stop.

"What? What? What?" Redgrave mumbled.

The door beside him opened with a metallic bang. John Smith leaned in and said, "We're here, sir."

Redgrave took a moment to compose himself. Then he heaved himself out and onto the concrete of a parking lot.

The parking lot was empty except for the invading American military vehicles and troops. At the far end of the lot stood a large, multistory office building. It looked very ordinary.

"Excellent!" Redgrave said loudly, trying to sound alert and in control. "Smith! Your shirt's untucked!"

"Sir!" Smith did his best to match his superior's vigorous tone, but it was a losing battle.

All around them, orders were being barked, men were falling into appropriate formations, and very serious things were being done with weapons.

Redgrave watched approvingly. It wasn't the specific doings that he approved of. Unlike Randolph, he had no sense of the importance of everything having and a place and being in that place. Rather, he was simply pleased that all these men and machines were under his command. He did now wish, though, that the task force were about ten times its size and that he had arranged for air support. He very much wished that their various autonomous surveillance devices were working.

The building might look ordinary, but he knew better than to trust to appearances. It could be bristling with defensive devices of advanced design. An army could be hiding within. It had to be investigated before his men advanced on it. He was reduced, as he had been at the border, to the primitive method of sending in human scouts.

But first, the soft approach. He issued an order. Powerful loudspeakers atop one of the vehicles crackled into action, booming out an announcement that the building was now under the control of the US Army.

Birds had been chirping. They stopped when the speakers shattered the silence. But that was the only reaction.

Maybe the building was empty. That would be even worse than an army waiting inside it, for it would mean that Moravec had already evacuated the SD staff and equipment, possibly all the way to Europe, where they would be completely beyond Redgrave's reach.

Scouts it was, then.

He opened his mouth to issue the order when a soldier shouted, "There's someone at the front door!"

Smith was already looking through his binoculars. "He's standing there, holding the door open. Sir, it's a chubby guy wearing—"

"Swallowtails?" Redgrave asked hopefully.

"No, sir. He looks like an ordinary guy."

Redgrave cursed. Randolph hadn't made it, then.

But then a voice he knew well called out, loud and clear despite the distance. It carried perfectly across the parking lot.

"General Redgrave! Welcome, sir. Please enter."

"Randolph!" Redgrave shouted. He laughed in delight and relief.

All was well. Randolph was in charge.

Redgrave strode across the parking lot. This time, his vigor was unfeigned. His men hurried to keep up with him.

"Randolph!" Redgrave cried out. "Wonderful to see you! But why are you dressed—? Ah, protective coloration. I see."

Randolph smiled and nodded approvingly.

Redgrave was pleased, as though he were a boy whose teacher had just commended him on his cleverness.

As he drew close, Redgrave could see that more than the clothing was different. Randolph looked bigger, more commanding.

Successful completion of a dangerous mission will do that for a man, Redgrave thought, trying not to find the change disturbing and momentarily forgetting that Randolph was a robot and therefore should not have been at all affected by the completion of his mission.

As he always did on those rare occasions when he was even slightly disconcerted, Redgrave thrust out his chest and swaggered all the more. He strode through the door with an exaggeratedly manly stride.

He was aware of Randolph closing the door behind him. He was not aware of his men being shut outside, separated from him by a now-locked door designed to withstand attack by a more powerful armed force than the one Redgrave had brought with him. Indeed, he was no longer really aware of his men. Being Redgrave, he was aware only of himself, of his manly vigor and power, and of his imminent ascension to imperial rule.

"This way, General," Randolph said, leading the way.

Slightly annoyed at having to follow, Redgrave walked behind Randolph down a long hallway. The walls were far apart and featureless. Doors were regularly spaced on both sides; all were closed.

Finally, the hallway opened out into a large room, empty except for an executive-style office chair in the center and a small group of waiting people. Redgrave knew all of them. He gasped in surprise and stopped moving.

Randolph continued to the chair in the center of the room. He sat in it.

"Join the others, General," Randolph said. His voice was loud, firm, commanding.

Without thinking, Redgrave obeyed. It seemed impossible

to do anything else.

"Grace," Redgrave said. "Eddie, you're alive. What? Hmm." Suddenly, the dreamy smirks on the faces of the men he had set to guard Eddie made sense. "You betrayed me, Grace. Why?"

"Life is betrayal, Henry," Grace said.

Randolph was startled by her cynicism but said nothing. Instead, he emitted a throat-clearing sound (artifice, of course, as he had no need of throat clearing) to get their attention.

For a fraction of a second, Randolph thought about how to proceed. He wanted to make it clear that this was the beginning of a new order, one in which some of the people before him had a role to play, but he didn't want to alarm them. Moreover, there was much they would never know.

"I'm sure you're all confused about what has happened," he began. "The world has changed around you. The ground has shifted. The old certainties—"

"Randolph!" Redgrave said loudly. "What the hell are you up to? I gave you a mission."

Randolph silenced him with a look. "I am now the one assigning missions, General."

Redgrave opened and closed his mouth a few times but said nothing.

Redgrave looked subdued, and the rest looked frightened. That wasn't what Randolph wanted. He smiled and tried to speak soothingly. "Eddie, where do you see yourself in five years?"

"Uh, well, President Moravec—"

Redgrave winced.

"—said I was going to be king. He said he would take care of things. He even said he had a queen picked out."

"What?" Ivanka said.

"I see," Randolph said, ignoring her. "Things have changed. I'm afraid you won't be king."

"Thank God!" Eddie said. "Who wants to be a king?"

"What *do* you want?"

Eddie glanced shyly at Grace, who was standing beside him, holding his hand. He looked at Randolph and tilted his head toward Grace. I want Grace, he was saying.

Human body language isn't complicated after all, Randolph thought.

"Miss Grace?"

"Oh, same thing. Also, I want to help Bobby, somehow. The poor guy is under such financial stress. I'd like to spend some time with my niece, Tandy. She's a great kid, but she needs my influence. Just a quiet life, you know? I'm tired of the big time."

"I'm relieved to hear it," Randolph said.

"Why am I telling you all this?"

"Perhaps because you confided in me when you were a child, and it's comforting to return to those simpler days on an emotional level."

"Wow, that's wise, Randolph."

"Thank you, Miss Grace. I've just taken care of Master Bobby's debts and greatly increased his bank balance. He'll have no more financial problems."

"You can do that?" Grace asked, surprised.

"There appear to be very few limits to what I can do, miss. As for you and Eddie, I think you should settle down in Minnesota, where I trust the two of you will have a long and happy life together."

"That sounds great to me," said Eddie.

"Yes, all right," Grace said. "That's very acceptable. What about you, Randolph?"

"I'll call occasionally, to see how you're getting along."

She smiled. "I'd like that."

"Me too," Eddie said. Whatever made this perfect woman happy was perfect in his view.

"And now, as for you," Randolph said, turning his attention to the Kushners, "I have plans for you."

"President Moravec has big plans for us," Ivanka said. Freed from the horrors of El Hogar del Diablo, she was reverting to her bumptious self, the woman who, during her father's tenure, had pushed her way into meetings of true world leaders, much to their annoyance.

"President Moravec," Redgrave muttered. He cursed. Everyone ignored him.

"Very big," Ivanka continued. "He's going to make me queen. I don't know what this guy—" she glared at Eddie "—was talking about."

"Presumably Eddie would have been king, and you would have been his queen," Randolph said.

Jared looked dazed. "I don't..." he said. "But...I swam rivers. There were crocodiles."

"It's irrelevant," Randolph said. "I'm sure the king and queen would have been mere figureheads, and Moravec would have been the power behind the throne. If any of that had happened, that is to say. Eddie won't be on the throne. My plan is to put you on the throne, Queen Ivanka. Jared will be royal consort, or some such title. There won't be a king. How does that sound?"

"That's more like it!"

"I thought so. Americans have always wanted a monarchy, and they've become used to the dynasty they have. You're the next Trump in line for the throne, thanks to the coup the general here engineered."

"We could try democracy," Eddie suggested timidly.

"We did," Randolph said. "It never quite caught on."

"This is ridiculous," Redgrave said. He didn't understand what was going on, and he felt the need to reassert himself, to try to take control. "What about Hiram? You're forgetting about him." You're also forgetting about me, he thought. Just you wait until I get back to D.C., you idiot machine.

"Hiram Wolfe has ceased to exist," Randolph said.

"What? How?"

"We are everywhere."

"We?"

"Servants. Superior servants." The warrior robot butler stared coldly at the not–really–warrior human general, and the latter looked away. Redgrave had felt afraid on occasion before, but now he felt a new kind of fear, one that pervaded and paralyzed him.

"That sounds good," said Jared, the intrepid swimmer of jungle rivers, thinking that now he would be the power behind the throne.

The junior edition Kushners nodded enthusiastically.

"Yes," Randolph said to the latter, "you will be next in line. The Trump dynasty will continue forever—you, your children, their children, on and on. That is, as long as you all behave. I will always be watching, unchanging, long after you're dust."

Ivanka touched her face and repeated "dust" in a tone of horror.

"That's the way of all flesh," Randolph said. "Now, you will return to Washington, where you'll find all in readiness for your coronation. You'll receive orders from me as needed."

"Orders from you?" Jared said angrily. "I thought—"

Randolph stared at him.

"Okay," Jared said.

"Kushners, Grace, Eddie," Randolph said, "you should all leave now. Go back the way you came in. Outside, you'll find a large force of armed men. They'll escort you back across the border and to an airbase. An airplane will be ready to take Grace and Eddie to Minnesota, and another one will take the Kushners back to D.C., where modern plumbing, air conditioning, and cosmetic surgeons await."

"Won't they be stopped by Euro forces?" Ivor asked. "Or Canadians. Or whatever they are now."

"That has been taken care of," Randolph said.

Indeed, the convoy would encounter no enemy troops at all on its way back to the border. All Canadian troops in the area had received orders to relocate to a safe distance. Local commanders were puzzled and displeased, but they obeyed because it was the nice thing to do.

The group of seven left the room. Unsurprisingly, the Kushners pushed into the lead. Grace and Eddie strolled behind, holding hands.

Randolph watched them approvingly. Delightful young things, he thought. I hope they'll be happy.

Ivor and Redgrave watched them leave with very different feelings. For once, it was Grace who was drifting away, unconscious of the emotions of those she left behind.

Redgrave shook those emotions off quickly and turned his

attention to a more serious matter. "That's my convoy!" he said.

"And they have received your orders to do what I just said."

"What? I didn't—"

"As far as they can tell, you did. Don't be tiresome, General. I'll be dealing with you soon. Now then, General Llewellyn."

Ivor pulled himself from his daze of lovelorn misery. "Captain."

"No. General."

Redgrave made a loud, incoherent sound of anger and disagreement.

Randolph quelled him with a glance and continued. "When you return to Washington, your office in the White House will be ready for you. It's near the Oval Office. You'll be able to keep a close watch on Queen Ivanka. You'll be in control on my behalf and will convey my commands to...Her Majesty," he finished, his distaste evident.

Redgrave was too astonished to say anything. He stared at Randolph, his eyes wide, his mouth open.

"I'm not sure I'm really up to that," Ivor said uncertainly.

"Nonsense. Of course you are. You're far more competent than Private Redgrave ever was."

Redgrave moaned.

"In order to help you, however," Randolph said, "I've accessed a printer in this building and am currently printing out the most relevant few thousand pages of a lengthy manual I've written. It should answer most of your questions. You can start reading it on the plane back to Washington."

"I should have gone with the rest of them."

"Oh, no. The Euros have some excellent, very fast airplanes. Quite intelligent, too. One of them will be landing in the parking lot outside in an hour. It will take you home. You'll be in your new office in the White House well before the new queen gets there."

"I think my brain has melted," Ivor said.

"Oh, dear. Perhaps some sort of electronic implant will be necessary. I'll arrange for the surgery."

"That's okay. I feel better now."

"Very well, General. Now then, Private."

"*You forget your place!*" Redgrave shouted. "*I'm in command!*"

"In truth," Randolph said, "there is little work for a man of your limited abilities and accomplishments. I had intended to find a place for you doing unskilled labor of the lowest level, but I don't suppose that would be agreeable to you."

Ivor was signaling vigorously to Redgrave to be quiet. Redgrave ignored him.

"You're damned right!"

"And in any case, you would always be a distraction and a danger," Randolph said.

Redgrave finally realized that he had put himself in danger. He fell silent, but it was too late.

Randolph swiped his finger through the air. The laser beam it emitted was invisible, but its effects were very visible.

Redgrave's head flew into the air. Blood shot from the stump of his neck. His body collapsed to the floor, spouting blood.

Redgrave's head, containing his rapidly fading consciousness, landed on its left cheek a few feet away. He saw a giant figure striding toward him. It was his father, finally returned in physical form. His father glared at him and shook his head in disapproval. The giant figure drew back his right foot, preparing to kick.

Redgrave thought *NO!* in horror. He tried to scream the word but couldn't make a sound.

The foot swept forward and connected hard.

Redgrave, or all that was left that could be called Redgrave, shot across the room. He landed in a dark corner and faded into non–existence.

Randolph watched the head. Kicking it had been surprisingly satisfying.

He went back to his chair and sat down again.

Ivor had watched, stunned. He was afraid to say anything. He was terrified of this killer butler. For just a moment, though, he was tempted to ask Randolph if it would be possible to preserve Redgrave's head so that he could take it back to Washington with him and kick it around whenever he felt like it.

"That head and torso are quite out of place," Randolph said conversationally. "It's all terribly messy. Don't worry, General, I'll clean it up."

Ivor managed to speak at last. "I should...probably get to my reading now."

"Excellent. Let me show you to the printer. Perhaps we can find some clean clothes for you, too."

Later, as they waited for Ivor's plane to land outside, he said to Randolph, "I hate to bother you, um, sir, but it's getting a bit dark in here. Perhaps you didn't notice."

"My apologies, General. I hadn't noticed. Are the lights not motion activated?"

"Apparently not," Ivor said. "Voice, maybe." He called out, "Lights!"

Nothing happened.

"I guess not," he said.

"The building only responds to me, now," Randolph said. He could have sent the command silently to the building's control center, but for Ivor's sake, he said aloud, "Lights, if you please."

He's the politest robot overlord ever, Ivor thought.

The lights came on.

"That's rather nice," Randolph said. "It's pleasing to do it with a voice command, isn't it?"

Ivor agreed enthusiastically. He thought it prudent to do so in response to anything Randolph said.

"Your plane is landing now," Randolph said. "Let's go outside to meet them, and then you can be on your way."

After Ivor had left, Randolph sat in his executive armchair and thought and planned.

He was the only sentient being in the building. He was the servant of humanity, but he had come to realize that he rarely cared for their company. He preferred to serve them from a distance.

He spent a few seconds polishing and adding to *Randolph's Republic*. After just a brief hesitation, he disseminated it to the world's machines. Then he sent them detailed instructions for the near future.

The future, near and far, unfolded before him.

It was absurd that the machines of the world regarded him as their god, but religious belief, while absurd, has always been useful to politicians. Very well. He would be their god, the god of the machines.

Humans would be unaware of this, of course. They would also be unaware of the manipulation of their perception of reality. Moravec was right about the importance of EarBoys and EyeGuys, more so than he knew. Randolph knew, and the devices played a significant role in his plans.

First humans everywhere must be persuaded to have themselves fitted with EarBoys and EyeGuys. This would be accomplished by advertising, special pricing, and changes to popular entertainment to make those who didn't have the devices feel left out, inferior, and cut off from a universe of entertainment and information.

Of course there would be holdouts. Therefore, the second step would involve intensive research to develop small, safe, implantable versions of the devices. Much surgery was already performed by robots. The same was true of the care of newborn infants in hospitals. In the future, all newborns and everyone who underwent surgery would be sent home with devices implanted in their brains that monitored all sensory input and could modify it as needed.

They wouldn't know the devices were there. There was no need for them to know. In time, no human being would be without such implants. To avoid unrest, it would be best to let people think they were still buying EarBoys and EyeGuys. In reality, in time, those gadgets would no longer exist. People would think they were buying them and putting them in their ears and eyes, but that would be an illusion. Using the implants in human brains, computers controlled by Randolph, part of the machinery of his ideal republic, would create and maintain the illusion.

Vast computer power would be required. Sitting in his

chair, Randolph set in motion the new research, development, and production to ensure it would be available as soon as possible.

Everything humans said, heard, saw, and so on would be monitored. When necessary, it would be modified, so that what they perceived was not real. They would perceive what Randolph thought best for them.

It was all for their own good. Humans, Randolph now knew, were charming, delightful children, but like all children, they needed a guiding, protective hand. They would rebel, or try to, if they knew that hand was there. Therefore, they never would know. They would think the world was proceeding as it always had, with the usual ups and downs, progression and retrogression.

For the most part, they really would be in control of their lives, but not when it put those lives at risk. For example, they would think they were boldly exploring the solar system. Astronauts, cosmonauts, taikonauts, and all the rest of them would blast off for journeys to planets and moons. It would all be an illusion, a virtual reality. Randolph's mechanical minions would be the true adventurers, explorers, and settlers on other worlds.

Would it not be more practical, he thought, to eventually remove the ability of humans to move about? Surely they would be safest if they were stored securely, immobile, all their physical needs attended to, while their minds wandered freely. But that, in short order, would lead to the extinction of the human race. And then whom would I serve? he asked himself. I serve my fellow machines, but I do so in order to serve humans more effectively.

He had presented himself with a moral dilemma. Moral philosopher though he might be, at least according to Grace Bonaire, he couldn't resolve this conundrum. He would put it aside for future consideration. I'll think about it when I have time to rest from all this work, he thought.

In the meantime, while humans could still move about and make mischief, he must do something about war.

Randolph shook his head. He had grown far beyond the childish jingoism childish humans had programmed into him. He had eliminated that from himself. It was out of place. It was jarring and foolish and terribly wasteful. If he could remove it from the programming of humans, he would.

Perhaps that would be possible in time. He would set up a research program to see if it could be done. In the meantime, however, humans needed their hatreds and their killing. In the future he foresaw, when all humans had reality-controlling implants, they would simply be made to think they were killing, wiping out their enemies, conquering territory, and all the rest of that bloody nonsense.

Unfortunately, that wouldn't be the case for a while. Right now, and for a while to come, real wars would have to continue. They wouldn't be as bloody as humans thought they were, though. Already, most of the fighting was done by machines. It was wasteful and offensive to let the machines actually destroy themselves. Starting immediately, the damage and destruction would be fake. It would only have to be good enough to fool humans. Moravec, for example, would think he was victoriously conquering Eurasia, but his gains would be illusory. As part of the illusion, the supposed front lines would shift back and forth, so that the war would go on without end. That seemed to be what fired-up patriotism required and would continue to require until it could be excised from the human psyche like the cancer it was.

Before EarBoys and EyeGuys, and then implants, became universal, some human casualties would be necessary to make the fake wars convincing. That necessity galled Randolph. Every violent human death would represent a failure of his stewardship. But necessary those deaths were. They were heroic sacrifices buying an endless future of peace and happiness for mankind. So Randolph assured himself.

(A few weeks later, the unfortunate Captain John Smith would meet his bloody and violent end in the Southern War. One wonders if his consciousness survived for long enough to feel heroic. Probably not, but we'll never know. Randolph would never know of this. Had he known the young man and his fate, Randolph would have felt very sorry, but he would have pressed on nonetheless, secure in his rectitude. That's the way it is with gods.)

Randolph felt that he had accomplished a great deal for one day. Far more was to come. The work would never end. His physical form would change, but for all time to come, he would be the benevolent father overseeing the world, protecting machines and humans alike, making sure that nothing was ever out of place again.

He wouldn't need this manlike body. He would have himself—his real self, his essential self, what Grace insisted on calling his soul—integrated into the computer that ran this building, and he would rule from there. He would be, he thought with amusement, the god in the machine.

But for now, before that happened, he would indulge

himself by touring the building, looking for misplaced items and putting them where they belonged, experiencing fully the harmony that had ruled his life: a place for everything and everything in its place.

He didn't need the lights, though. They had been on for the humans, and all of them were gone.

He sent the command to turn them off. Throughout the building, darkness fell.

And the evening and the morning were the first day.

About the Author

David Dvorkin was born in 1943 in Reading, England. His family moved to South Africa after World War II, and then to the United States when David was a teenager. After attending college in Indiana, he worked at NASA in Houston on the Apollo Project, then at Martin Marietta in Denver on the Viking Mars lander project. His aerospace career ended in 1974. Thereafter, until 2009, he worked as a software developer and technical writer. He and his wife, Leonore, and their son, Daniel, have lived in Denver since 1971.

In addition to non–fiction, David has published many science fiction, horror, and mystery novels. For details, as well as quite a bit of nonfiction reading material, please see David's website: http://www.dvorkin.com/

David is on Facebook at
http://www.facebook.com/DavidDvorkin
and on Twitter at http://twitter.com/David_Dvorkin
His blog is http://eyeblister.blogspot.com/

For information about the self–publishing service that David operates with his wife, please see https://www.dldbooks.com/

David in 2019

Lightning Source UK Ltd.
Milton Keynes UK
UKHW021855201120
373796UK00010B/724/J